NO ROOM FOR LOVE

There had to be a way to reach out to his parents and bring the heart back into Christmas.

by Stella Whitelaw

IT had been a strange year for Peter Miller, aged six. It was the year his daddy left home and his mother cried a lot, snapped at Peter and lost her fair prettiness. Peter did not fully understand why his daddy should leave their nice home, but he felt vaguely guilty that it was his fault.

He remembered that he had been extremely naughty that last Christmas. Peter had woken at the unearthly grey hour of five, heart pounding with excitement.

He had opened his stocking, eaten all the sweets, and bounced into his parents' room where they were still asleep.

All morning he had pestered them to open the presents, frazzling their frayed nerves, refusing to eat his dinner, and then being very slightly sick on Mum's best dress.

Mum had cried into the cooling rum sauce, but Peter was not quite sure whether it was because of the stain on her dress or because Dad was upstairs throwing all his clothes into suitcases.

This Christmas, Peter was going to be very, very careful. Besides, he was to play the part of the innkeeper in the school Nativity play. Miss Lawson had told him he was a head taller than anyone else in the class, and it would "bring him out of himself."

It was true Peter didn't want to speak to people quite so much now. He didn't understand why his dad no longer lived at home. He saw him on strange, unreal occasions when they traipsed round the zoo or museums on a Saturday morning, ate in cafés, and then rushed back to Mum as if Peter was a parcel that had to be delivered on time.

His mum and dad barely spoke to each other at the door, and that was upsetting.

Peter knew that his mum was having a hard time. She was trying to be both a mum and dad to him, and she was always tired.

He found her crying over a plug she couldn't fix on the new toaster, and he stood there, pulling at his Superman T-shirt. At six, what could he do? He didn't know how to fix the toaster either. It was something his

dad had always done.

The rehearsals for the Nativity play seemed to take up more time than lessons at school. Now that Peter had twigged that it was going to be like television, he learned his lines and practised them earnestly.

Each morning and evening he said them in the bathroom while cleaning his teeth.

"Go away," he said through a mouthful of toothpaste. "We're full up. There's no room at the inn."

He watched himself in the mirror, white-lipped and obstinate, wondering if he was the baddie of the show. Everything on television was divided into goodies and baddies.

Perhaps it was the same with a Nativity play.

"Is that all you have to say?" his mum asked, looking up from her ironing board.

She had taken the ironing upstairs so that she could supervise Peter's bedtime routine at the same time as ironing.

She had a full-time job now, and all the housework had to be done in the evenings.

"Miss Lawson says it's a very important part," Peter said, spitting foam round the basin. "She says it's cru . . . cru . . ."

"Crucial?"

"That's right. Very important. She says it's a miracle play."

"And so it is," his mum said, folding his sweatshirt precisely. She had always folded Daddy's shirts like this and now she did it for Peter.

"Are you coming to the play?" Peter asked.

"Of course," his mum said. "Wouldn't miss it for the world." She hesitated for a moment, and then in a bright voice added, "Your daddy and I are both coming."

Peter knew that already. He'd heard his mum on the telephone.

"Jeffrey, you *have* to be at the Nativity play," she had said. "You can't let Peter down. He's your son and you have to be there.

"I don't really care how busy you are at work," she'd gone on, containing her fury into an icy calm. "Surely you can spare one afternoon? Your son, Peter, is taking a leading role, and if you're not there to see him, it'll break his heart. He may be a part of the homelife that you say was stifling you, but he's also your son."

Peter didn't know what stifling meant but he knew it wasn't good.

There was quiet for a moment as his mum listened to his dad.

"Please come," and this time the anger was gone, and somehow that made her voice even sadder. "No, it won't unsettle him to see us together . . ."

"OK, then, two o'clock on the last Friday of term. Peter needs you . . ."

She'd put down the phone and leaned against the wall. Peter could see her hands shaking. She rubbed her eyes and one solitary tear rolled down her cheek.

P ETER continued rehearsing his role with solemn carefulness. He had grown more solemn and more careful. He must do nothing wrong this year. Life was not all fun, he had learned. It could be quite awful, and it was even more awful if one did not understand why. His mother was so soft and pretty, so why had his daddy gone away?

The dress rehearsal of the Nativity play was exciting. Peter enjoyed dressing up in an old sheet dyed brown with instant coffee and a striped towel round his head held in place with rope.

He felt very grand and six feet tall like his daddy. He just needed a finishing touch.

"Can I have a beard?" he asked Miss Lawson.

"No, dear," Miss Lawson said. "You have to be clean shaven."

"But why can't I have a beard?" Peter persisted.

"Because you're the baddie, you're the baddie, you're the baddie, stupid," shrieked Terence Browning, who was playing Joseph.

He had been given the part of Joseph because he had a good memory and a mother who did not work and could spend hours going over his lines.

He had learned his words in one continuous string, and once switched on it was difficult to stop him. He was full of confidence and bounce, and couldn't wait for the performance.

Peter dropped his gaze from the school make-up box, letting the dreaded news sink in. Of course, he was the baddie.

He sent Mary away. He sent Joseph away. He let that poor little baby be born in a smelly old stable among the pigs and cows.

He was awful, rotten, no wonder no-one liked him. It merely reinforced the rôle he felt he had played in his parents' break-up.

His mother helped Peter all she could with his part, giving him the cue lines as he cleaned his teeth.

"Go away," Peter snarled. "We're full up. There's no room at the inn."

"Very, very good," his mum said, giving his brow a brief kiss. "You're going to be a knock-out as the innkeeper."

"You are going to be there tomorrow, aren't you? And Daddy?" Peter had to be sure. It was so important that they should both be there, seeing him as a person, real, taking part in something that they had no part in. School was his world.

"Of course we'll be there," his mum said, folding his innkeeper's robe into a carrier bag. "I've got the afternoon off. And Dad said he'd come. I'll get there early for a good seat. Don't worry, darling, we'll both be there."

Next day the nervous excitement in the classroom used as a dressing-room was electric. Peter put on his outfit. He did look a very dashing figure in the mirror provided.

If only he could wear some of that crinkly hair they were sticking on to the youthful chin of Terence.

"No, Peter." Miss Lawson was adamant. "I've told you before. You can't have a beard. Only Joseph and the shepherds have beards."

"But, Miss Lawson, if Mary and Joseph came to the inn late in the evening, and the inn was full up and the innkeeper had been busy all day, he wouldn't have had time to shave, would he?" Peter said, using the kind of logic his dad often threw at Mum.

Miss Lawson, looking frustrated, gave in.

Peter happily applied a sinister five o'clock shadow with a dark pencil, rubbing it vigorously into his skin. If he was the baddie, then he was jolly well going to look like one.

THE Nativity play was in full flight. Miss Lawson was looking pleased as the shepherds sat around their fire, crunching crisps and looking everywhere for the star. Several saw it in different directions. Then the angel, Gabriel, appeared, resplendent in a white sheet and wired tinsel wings and halo.

"Behold, I am Gabriel," he declared angelically.

Peter took a deep breath as they came to his scene and strode purposefully out of the door of his inn to confront the travellers.

He glanced at the audience, surprised to see a vast sea of faces all looking at him expectantly, rows of eyes riveted on him. It was totally unnerving.

He froze with fright. His body turned to stone. Not a single word came to his lips. His mind was a complete blank.

He stared at the swimming, moon-shaped faces. He hardly recognised Miss Lawson in the wings, making frantic signals to him.

Suddenly, his mother's face swam into focus. Why was she looking so anxious? Peter was vaguely aware that his father was sitting beside her, blond and serious, leaning forward as if to catch something.

His mother began to mime the action of cleaning her teeth and the words snapped into Peter's head.

"Go away," he said tonelessly. "We're full up. There's no room at the inn."

"But my wife is heavy with child and the baby will be born tonight. We are weary and cannot walk any further. You cannot be so cruel as to turn us away," Terence declaimed, with the assurance of one who knew his words perfectly.

He was holding on to Mary with a proprietary air.

"Go away," Peter snarled. This was not acting. He didn't like Terence at all. "We're full up. There's no room at the inn."

"But we've come a long way," Joseph argued. "And we are both tired. Mary is about to give birth. We must have a place to rest."

Miss Lawson had given the part of Mary to little Missie Clark. She was a thin, pale child with straight brown hair and huge dark eyes. She certainly looked as if she had travelled from afar on the back of a donkey.

S HE was an obedient pupil and followed stage directions implicitly. She had nothing to say; she merely had to follow whoever led. What Miss Lawson did not know was that Missie Clark could really act. As Peter opened his mouth to send Mary and Joseph aggressively on their way once and for all, to banish them to the lowly stable among the animals, Missie happened to look up at him.

Her dark eyes were brimming with tears and, as Peter watched, fascinated, two tears hovered on her lashes like early-morning dew drops, quivered, then rolled slowly down her pale cheeks.

Peter felt a wave of compassion sweeping through his body, melting the ice that had encased his heart all year. The warmth brought a feeling of joy and happiness that he had to share.

He smiled down at Mary, her young but care-worn face framed by a rough blue shawl. He was unaware of anyone else on the stage. Only the two of them seemed to exist.

"Don't worry, Mary," Peter said, his voice ringing with conviction across the school hall. "You can have my room. I'll go and sleep in the stable."

From that moment, the Nativity play disintegrated. It was more terrible than Miss Lawson's worst nightmare. The three Wise Men, painfully confused, began to argue in loud voices about what to do next; two of the lambs were fighting over the baby Jesus in the manger. One of the angels began flapping her wings energetically around the stage, having a lovely time on her own and getting in everyone's way; Joseph was howling for his mother — he still had his best lines to say.

Peter and Missie walked off stage unnoticed in the chaos and were halfway across the playground before Missie stopped crying.

Peter was not sure if Missie was really having a baby, but he put his arm round her thin shoulders protectively just in case.

He felt ten feet tall. He had done the right thing. Christmas was about kindness and love for other people. He knew his parents would approve.

Back in the school hall, the audience collapsed into helpless laughter as the set piece on stage fell apart at the seams. Shepherds, lambs and angels were all doing their own thing. They were rushing about, pushing, shouting, squaring up private fights and grievances, swopping bits of costume and finishing off the crisps.

Miss Lawson stood in the wings, stunned and open-mouthed. Where had she gone wrong?

"Never mind, Miss Lawson," the caretaker said, who was standing by to sweep up the stage. "You got 'em laughing, and that can't be bad."

Susan and Jeffrey were in fact laughing so much they did not notice that they were clutching at each other's hands for support. It seemed to unlock a door that had been bolted and corroded with rust. They began, hesitatingly, to talk, becoming two more people oblivious to those around them.

"I haven't laughed . . . so much . . . for months," Jeffrey said, shaking his head and grinning.

"For years," Susan said.

"I've been so stupid, haven't I?" His eyes, so much like Peter's, were troubled. "My family should come first, not my work. It was just the pressure, you see . . .

"I know I've treated you both badly. What can I say? I don't know. I don't know how to talk to you any more."

"This is talking," Susan said gently.

"I know I'm asking a lot, but can you be very, very patient with me? It's like . . . it's like getting over an illness."

Susan thought of the past year, the hardship, the loneliness. It would not be easy to forget. Perhaps she could never forget. She thought of how Peter had suffered, not even understanding what had happened and why, and all the sharp things she had planned to say to Jeffrey.

"Are you going to tell me to go away?" Jeffrey asked. "Like the innkeeper?"

Susan remembered the glow on Peter's face as he changed the course of history with a few simple words from his heart, and she could not help smiling.

PETER brought Missie to the door of the hall. There was a chill late afternoon wind blowing across the playground and more than a hint of snow in the leaden sky. He did not want her to catch cold. He caught sight of his parents talking together, their heads close, and he could hardly believe his eyes. They were looking at each other as they had in the old, happy days.

Miss Lawson had said it was a miracle play and she'd been right. He must remember to tell her. She would be pleased.

"Mum . . . Dad," Peter said. "This is Missie Clark."

Susan drew the children into the circle of her love. A small boy, aged six, had shown her the way.

She did not need to say the lines she had rehearsed to say to Jeffrey. They were not necessary now and she might never say them. Instead she would speak from her heart.

Perhaps she could not change history, but she might change the future. ∎

Trust In Me

by Joyce Begg

She'd reminded people that she was capable, efficient and dependable once too often. Now they'd forgotten she could be vulnerable, too.

T'S January 1 and, since Tony was good enough to give me this beautiful diary for Christmas, the least I can do is start it off. I haven't kept a diary since I was 12, when the entries were of such earth-moving significance as: *Today it rained. Hockey postponed. Sausages for tea* — all jammed into a space two inches by one.

This diary allows for much longer entries because you mark in your own dates. Does that make it a journal?

It has a clasp and a lock, too. Dear knows what secrets Tony imagines that I have.

However, since it does have a lock, I feel safe in committing to black and white my New Year resolution.

It is this: If I don't meet someone special before my 35th birthday, I'll blow all my savings on a holiday cruise.

That gives me five months.

Writing that down on page one of my lovely new diary will lend purpose to my mission.

Mind you, I quite fancy a cruise. Norwegian fjords, I think.

January 2.

Things have not got off to a good start. The drawback about being a live-in housekeeper/receptionist/secretary is that I don't meet many people of *any* description, far less eligible males.

Plenty of visitors come to the house, of course; or at least to the surgery. But they are usually accompanied by a dog with mange or a poorly cat — or they leave a message that a horse at the riding stables has got worms.

Not really the stuff of romance.

Anyway, the surgery is closed today to all but emergencies. I am alone here.

I quite enjoy being on my own, especially in my flat over the garage. It's small, bright, comfortable and very tempting on a cold January day, when there's a good film on telly . . .

But that attitude won't help me in my long-term plans.

Tony is off to Winterford to see Samantha, his latest girlfriend. I must stop feeling responsible for Tony all the time. After all, he's 17 and he will be off to university in the autumn, or so he hopes.

This is another reason for my pressing ahead with my plans. Whatever he says, Richard will no longer need a live-in housekeeper once his son goes. He'll be able to cope by himself then.

It was different when the twins were still around, last year. But now we only see them when the mood takes them. At the moment, they're skiing in Austria.

I was needed at Christmas, of course. Sometimes I feel I earn a month's salary on Christmas Day alone.

12

Richard is out checking on a sheep that has got its hind leg jammed down a rabbit hole.

February 14

Tony has sent me a Valentine card. He says it wasn't him, but I know no-one else who would spend £2.50 on a velvet heart and then borrow money from me to go to a concert.

I don't expect a card from Richard. After all, he's my employer — and about as romantic as a door-stop.

Also, I imagine that if he thinks of anyone on Valentine's Day, it will surely be his ex-wife, Frances. She's living in Seattle now, with an engineer.

A good-looking if slightly craggy man brought an Alsatian to the surgery this morning. His name is Teddington (the man, not the Alsatian) and he's moved into the old cottage on Main Street that's been empty for six months.

Late 30s, dark hair with just a sprinkling of grey above the ears. The word is that he's a sanitary inspector. He looks all right to me. I am not proud about that kind of thing.

I wonder if he plays badminton. If he's just moved in, he won't know about the local clubs and activities.

He's coming back for an injection next week (for the Alsatian). Maybe I'll mention the badminton club. They could use some decent men.

I wonder why he's not married.

February 25

He's not a sanitary inspector, he's a *rock climber*! A *professional* rock climber. I didn't think that was possible.

Apparently he has never married because his lifestyle is fraught with hazards and he doesn't expect a woman to put up with that.

It simply wouldn't be fair to leave a wife behind all the time.

I admire his sentiments, but can't help thinking how proud I'd be to marry a policeman or fireman, who bravely face danger every day.

Although he hasn't played badminton before, he's a natural athlete. His hand and eye co-ordination is fantastic. So's his sense of humour — not a common characteristic in rock climbers, I should imagine.

Richard had to put a cat to sleep this afternoon. He has to do it quite often but he always hates it. This was Mrs Maxwell's tabby, Marzipan.

Maybe Mrs Maxwell would like one of Marianne's kittens. I'm trying to find homes for them all. I must check with Tony.

Picked up a batch of brochures at the travel agent's this morning.

March 18 and I have a date! Alistair Teddington has asked me if I'd like to go to a concert of Tudor music at the cathedral.

It's not exactly dinner at the Ritz, but at least it shows he has taste — I think.

The thing is, I'm not sure if this is a *proper* date, or if he just asked me because he thought I might be interested. In the music, I mean.

I'll wear my blue wool suit. It has both glamour *and* comfort. The cathedral can be pretty draughty.

Richard has been a touch bad-tempered this week. You'd think he'd be nicer to everyone, what with his birthday coming up next month and everything.

Maybe that's the problem. I think he's going to be 44.

I don't know what to get him. He did mention a book on rare diseases in cattle but I can't imagine he wants it for his birthday.

I'll see what Tony says. That way I can remind him diplomatically at the same time. Tony's attention has been entirely taken up with Felicity recently.

I sometimes wonder, is Tony's mania for changing girlfriends every three weeks normal? Is he trying to compensate, somehow, for his mother leaving home four years ago? What would she — Frances — have done?

Should I nag him more about his homework, or would that have a negative effect? Is it any of my business?

Fancy a rock climber being interested in Tudor music. I hope it's not too awful.

March 29

The music was fabulous. Sort of eerily beautiful. Alistair has opened up a whole new field of interest for me.

He took me for a pizza after the concert. Again, hardly the Ritz, but then I don't expect rock climbers earn much.

I've bought Richard a deerstalker, complete with ear flaps. He is out at all times and in all conditions and he's an idiot about simple protection from the elements.

He thinks he's immortal. He says he never catches anything, like those doctors who deal in all sorts of diseases and develop a resistance to them.

I tell him that he may never come down with foot-and-mouth, but is just as likely to catch colds as the rest of us mortals.

He is still behaving like a bear. It must be overwork. I hope he'll like the deerstalker.

Tony had a look at the brochures I have been collecting. He suggested the Greek islands. I've kind of gone off the notion of a cruise just at the moment.

April 5

Richard said he was "delighted" with the deerstalker. I think "bemused" would be a closer description.

He looked positively dashing in it. It makes him seem taller and gives him a keen-and-intelligent look into the bargain, like a bloodhound on the scent.

I showed him how to tie the earflaps, but he said he'd wear them either on top of his head or loose. I think that was because I said he looked sweet with the bow under his chin.

He did, though. He was transformed from a bloodhound into a King Charles spaniel in one move. I hadn't noticed how dark his eyes are. Really deep brown.

Because of Richard's birthday I had to turn down Alistair's invitation to the cinema tonight. Must admit I didn't thrill to the idea of a Polish classic in sub-titles, anyway.

Even Tony put off going out with Felicity. He said it was just because it was his dad's birthday. But I think the steak Diane and the Black Forest gâteau may have had something to do with it.

I've arranged to go out with Alistair next Saturday instead.

April 12

What a wonderful day! I think there's a very good chance I may fall in love with Alistair in the near future.

We went for a long walk this afternoon, right round the end of the lake. The sun was brilliant, the breeze light, the grass spring-green.

Attilla (Alistair's Alsatian) ran round like a mad thing. Anyone would think he'd been chained up in a cellar for weeks.

Alistair says it's because he's missing the climbing. He goes along quite often.

Alistair has spent the last six months writing up his notes on climbing in Snowdonia, and hopes to have the book in print by Christmas. It's all very impressive.

We passed Richard at one point, or rather he passed us in the van on a farm track. He nodded at us in such a bad-tempered way, I thought the clutch might be playing up again — or maybe it was last night's chilli con carne.

I didn't change the recipe, and it's never bothered him before. But I suppose something in it could have given him heartburn.

April 19

Too tired to write much. Spent all day spring-cleaning, then Alistair and I went out for a curry.

I left a salad for Richard and Tony. I've stopped giving Richard spicy food. His moods seem to be getting worse. It can't all be overwork.

I hope the curry doesn't give me heartburn as well. Alistair was very entertaining. I can't remember a thing he said, but we laughed all evening.

April 26

I'm thinking of resigning. If Richard wasn't so busy, I'd be off like a shot. I am almost unconscious with fatigue.

As it is, I'm going to insist on a mobile phone. This running to answer the thing every three minutes may be good for the heart but it's a strain on the nerves and exhausting on the legs. The thing never stops.

It wouldn't be so bad if I didn't have a basket of kittens, a sick canary and a month-old lamb in the utility room, all calling for attention.

All I need now is for Richard to bring home a calf.

I suppose there's room in the garage . . .

I'm so tired I can't think properly about my new year resolution. All I know is, I have less than one month left. Alistair is being most attentive . .

WHAT a beginning to the month of May!

I am writing this just after midnight on May 2 because, although I'm physically whacked and emotionally wrung, I know I won't be able to sleep.

The day started before breakfast with Eric Sheridan phoning from Upper Finchott Farm. One of his cows was in danger of losing her calf. I handed Richard a toasted bacon sandwich and he vanished, earflaps waving.

The lamb in the utility-room was making such a din that I warmed up his milk early.

Two of the kittens jumped out of the basket and tried to knock him over, eager to drink from his bottle. But I wasn't about to start feeding six kittens when they have a perfectly good mother.

Anyway, I have almost weaned them on to mince.

At nine o'clock, I was able to sit down and have a cup of coffee and four bites of toast. Then the phone rang. It was Stephanie, wondering whether Tony was going to Winterford with her or not.

At weekends, Tony doesn't surface till around three in the afternoon, except for something pretty critical, like Bugs Bunny on telly.

I passed on his excuses and Stephanie said she'd see him later.

At 9.15 I decided I couldn't put off washing the curtains in the twins' bedroom any longer. I took them down and put them into the automatic.

It was while I was Hoovering under their beds that Tony appeared in his nightshirt, his eyes still shut.

He said somebody had just phoned about a goldfish developing black-spot, but he couldn't remember the name.

While he retired to his room again and crashed out, I gave up Hoovering. I had to be able to hear the phone.

I was afraid that the next emergency could be a dying horse, and then we'd be in real trouble.

At 10.20, Jimmy Davidson, aged nine, phoned to say his gerbil was looking peculiar. I promised that just as soon as the calf was born, Richard would have a look at the gerbil — providing nothing more vital happened in between.

At 10.30 I set about the twins' bedroom carpet with two gallons of shampoo. This little exercise took 45 minutes (if I allow for four phone calls).

It left the carpet clean but rather more soggy than I would have liked.

I opened the windows wide, and carried the bucket back downstairs.

At 11.25, Mrs Maxwell called to choose a kitten to replace the late Marzipan. She didn't like any of Marianne's kittens. (This is a different batch.)

While we were in the utility-room examining the kittens, the lamb decided it might as well have something to drink. I heated more milk.

Mrs Maxwell took 35 minutes to decide which kitten she wanted. And as I finally ushered her out of the front door, assuring her that I would let her know the minute the kitten was ready to leave its mother, the twins walked in.

They had come home for the weekend, and couldn't understand why I was not ecstatic to see them. I tried to keep cool.

"You'll have to sleep in the study," I said — which, now I look back on it, was not the warmest welcome they had ever received.

I might have made it warmer had the phone not rung.

At 12.30, Richard returned, looking pinched around the gills.

I set a bowl of nourishing vegetable soup for him on the kitchen table, and just saved it from being devoured by a twin.

The phone rang. Jimmy Davidson. The gerbil was looking much better.

AT two o'clock the rain came on and I had to take in the curtains. They were still damp, so I stuck them in the tumble-drier and shrank them. The twins said the house was cold, so I went to investigate and, sure enough, the boiler had gone out. It took 24 minutes to get it going again. When I emerged from the cellar (covered in smudges from head to toe, my hair like a black dandelion clock) it was to find Alistair and Attilla in the kitchen waiting for me.

I couldn't have looked less glamorous if I had been a 20-stone lady wrestler.

He smiled as though I was Posh Spice. I thought I detected the faintest palpitation, but I couldn't be sure.

I made everyone cups of tea (having washed my hands but not my face — I hadn't realised how bad it was) and sat down for five minutes.

The phone rang, but one of the twins answered it.

Alistair, looking even more craggy and magnificent than usual, said he had come to tell me he was off to the Cairngorms for 10 days.

I said I would miss him, and he returned the compliment.

"You'll have company, though," he said.

I thought of the utility-room and its assorted occupants, not to mention Tony and the twins. Then I sent a twin up to waken Tony while I remembered.

"Oh, yes, I'll have company all right."

"You mean you'll do it? Good girl. I knew you wouldn't let me down. Thanks ever so much."

"Do what?"

He looked blank.

"Look after Attilla for me. Isn't that what we're talking about?"

"I must have missed that bit."

"But you'll do it, won't you? He's dead easy to look after. As long as he's fed, he's as gentle as a lamb."

"Just don't open the utility-room door, Alistair," I said, as the dog ambled towards it. "There's a lamb already in there."

"Is there?"

"And six kittens and a sick canary."

"Fancy that."

The utility-room door opened, Richard came through it and Attilla went in.

In one swift movement, Richard swung round to reach for the dog, but his tiredness was telling, and the Alsatian slipped past him.

There followed several minutes of pandemonium — during which the kittens retreated screeching to their box, the cat spat furiously, the lamb had hysterics and the canary almost expired.

Actually, I don't think Attilla would have harmed any of them.

Alistair had stood open-mouthed in the kitchen all this time.

"As you can see, Alistair, I couldn't possibly keep Attilla," I breathed once we were back in the kitchen with the door shut.

"But there's no-one else," he replied mournfully. "How else can I do the Cairngorms?"

Richard said nothing, but turned away to pour himself a large cup of very strong, hot tea.

I don't know what embarrassed me more, Alistair's incredible selfishness, or his arrogance. How can anyone "do" the Cairngorms?

Within 10 minutes I had sent him packing, retired to the flat, had a good cry, and got out all my cruise brochures.

That was how Richard found me half an hour later. He had taken three telephone calls and answered the door twice.

I had still not looked in a mirror and, as I found out later, my tears had now added to the wreckage of my general appearance.

"Come in," I said in answer to his knock.

He looked almost as bad as I did, only he was pale and tired and still had on his deerstalker.

"Are you all right?" he asked.

"You knew he was a creep all the time, didn't you?"

"No, of course I didn't. I didn't *like* him but —" He sighed, sat down on the sofa, and started to laugh feebly.

"I wish I'd knocked him down. I was so mad I could have broken his nose. I should have done. I was just too exhausted."

That didn't seem the moment to point out that Alistair was twice his size and that if he'd laid a finger on him, Attilla would have eaten him.

"Why were you mad?"

He looked at me for several minutes with those deep brown eyes.

"Which reason would you like first? The one about huge dogs cavorting about among small animals? Or the one about him trying to exploit your kindness?

"Or the one about him making me feel awful because I've taken you for granted, too?

"Or the one about him taking a place in your affections that I wanted so much and which he was taking away from me?"

There was silence for 45 seconds at least. And then, "Pardon?" I said.

"I'm not going to say all that again," he declared.

"The last bit will do."

So he said the last bit again, and quite a bit more, and the result was that he got himself covered in smudges and I got palpitations.

I've covered 10 pages of the diary but I might not have time to write anything else till the middle of June.

I have to think seriously about which cruise Richard and I should go on, once his busy season ends.

Tony still thinks the Greek islands, the twins think Madeira, but I still prefer the Norwegian fiords.

What could be more romantic for a honeymoon than the Norwegian fiords? ∎

THE NEST

by Joyce Stranger

Inspired by an illustration by Mark Viney

In the middle of a field
In a grass built dome
A tiny mouse
Has made her home.
Each broad-leaved blade
With precision set
To keep her safe
From the cold and wet.

Here in the midst of the standing corn
One summer night, her babes were born.

In the distant farm on a summer day
They plan to take the corn away.
The tractors come and the hard earth shakes
Terrified, the small mouse quakes.
She knows that she each babe must save
Or her well built nest will become their grave.

She travels the field in frantic haste
Her young in her mouth, in a desperate race.
At the side of the field, against the hedge,
She lays each one on a tiny ledge.

The giant wheels crush the minute dome,
But when morning comes she's rebuilt her home.
Her family lies on a sheepwool bed,
Each one safe and newly fed.

The corn is cut, the field is clear
The mice survive for the rest of the year.

NO MORE WAS

Chase away your wash-day blues with
our matching peg and laundry bags made from brightly-coloured fabrics.

Our bags are made from sturdy striped cotton fabric and decorated with a cord washing line and appliquéd washing. A friendly sun beams down on the washing made from a circle of embroidered felt with a button decoration. The finished bags are slipped over coat hangers so they can be hung anywhere, and will prove to be a practical addition to any household.

PEG BAG

WHAT YOU NEED:

Paper and pencil
Coat hanger
Ruler
Saucer
Scissors
Striped cotton base fabric
Cotton lining
Dressmaker's chalk pencil
Fusible bonding
Felt and fabric scraps
Iron
Sewing thread and pins
Piping cord
Button for the sun
Stranded embroidery cotton (floss)
Embroidery needle
Calico
Fabric marker pen

1 To make a paper pattern for the peg bag, measure the width of the coat hanger, add 2 cm (¾ in) to this measurement, then draw a rectangle equal to this width and 42 cm (16½ in) long. For the opening, place a saucer centrally 5 cm (2 in) from one short edge, then draw around it. Place the coat hanger along the top of this short edge, then draw around the curved shape and mark the position of the hook. Add a 1.5 cm (⅝ in) seam allowance all the way round the pattern. Cut out the circle for the opening.

2 Cut the pattern twice from striped cotton fabric without cutting out the hole — one for the front and one for the back. Make sure the stripes run the same way on both pieces. Cut a third piece from cotton lining. Pin the striped front to the lining piece with right sides facing. Lay the pattern on top and use a chalk pencil to draw the opening on the lining; remove the pattern. Machine stitch round the line, then cut the fabric away from the centre, 1.5 cm (⅝ in) from the stitching line. Clip into the seam allowances for ease, then turn the lining through the hole to the wrong side. Press, then topstitch around the edge of the hole.

3 Trace one shirt, one pair of trousers and two socks from our templates onto fusible bonding. Iron the bonding onto the wrong side of fabric scraps and cut out the shapes.

Continued on page 24.

Continued from page 22.
Peel away the backing and arrange the shapes on the striped front. Iron the shapes to fuse them in place, then secure them with machine or hand-stitching.

4 Stitch a length of piping cord, knotted at each end, above the washing, then stitch on a circle of felt for the sun, slightly larger than your button.

Taken from THE SCRAP CRAFT PROJECT BOOK by Nicki Wheeler, published by David & Charles.
Text and designs Copyright © Nicki Wheeler 1998
Photography and layout Copyright © David & Charles 1998

Stitch the button to the centre of the circle, then use embroidery cotton (floss) and straight stitch to add the sun's rays and the pegs holding the washing on the line.

5 Cut a small calico patch and write 'PEGS' on it using a fabric marker pen. Iron the patch on the wrong side to fix the writing, then machine stitch it to the striped front about 1 cm (⅜ in) from the edges. Tease out the threads on the edges of the calico to fray them.

6 Pin, then tack the front and back bag pieces together with right sides facing. Stitch around all four edges taking a 1.5 cm (⅝ in) seam allowance and leaving a 2.5 cm (1 in) gap at the top for the hook of the coat hanger. Trim the seam allowances at the corners. Turn the bag right sides out and insert the coat hanger through the opening. Fill the bag with pegs.

LAUNDRY BAG

WHAT YOU NEED:

Paper and pencil
Strong coat hanger
Ruler
Scissors
Striped cotton base fabric
Cotton lining
Dressmaker's chalk pencil
Fusible bonding
Felt and fabric scraps
Iron
Sewing thread and pins
Piping cord
Three buttons
Stranded embroidery cotton (floss)
Embroidery needle
Calico
Fabric marker pen

1 Measure the width of the coat hanger, add 2 cm (¾ in) to this measurement, then draw a rectangle on the paper equal to this width and 62 cm (241/2 in) long. For the opening, draw a large oval shape centrally 5 cm (2 in) from one short edge with the chalk pencil. (You may find it easiest to draw around a small oval serving dish, if you have one.) Place the coat hanger along the top of this short edge, then draw around the curved shape and mark the position of the hook.
Add a 1.5 cm (⅝ in) seam allowance all the way round. Cut out the oval for the opening.

2 Follow steps 2-6 for the peg bag to assemble the bag but add some extra washing so you have two shirts, one pair of trousers and four socks. Stitch a button to each end of the washing line and write 'LAUNDRY' on the calico rectangle instead of 'PEGS'.

"Tell Me What

You See..."

How ironic that after years of dreaming about her very special place, she was going back to see it — through someone else's eyes . . .

by Eileen Elias

THE sun was shining. Kate Bentley, standing at the open window of her little room, felt the blessed warmth of it on her face and knew it was the answer to her prayer.

Only the night before, Kate had lain awake, listening to the steady drumming of rain on the roof. Rain, remorseless, unceasing. Rain in June.

Summers aren't what they used to be, she reflected. When she and Arthur were children in Elbury, it never seemed to rain in summertime.

But that was many years ago. Everything was different now, even the weather.

Tomorrow was the day of the outing; the trip to the country that young Norah had promised her. The day she had been longing for, when she would see again her view from the hill.

For a while her spirits sank. She would never really "see" that view of Elbury again.

Now that her sight had gone, only in her mind's eye could she hope to follow the

27

downward curve of the road, the line of the little street, the slender church tower embowered in trees.

All that could be only a memory now.

Still, the chance had come to breathe the freshness of the air and listen to the country sounds and that was an opportunity she couldn't miss.

She had lost track of distances; it was so long since she had ventured far afield. And for a little while she'd been afraid it was too far for young Norah to drive. But she'd been reassured on that score.

And now in answer to her little prayer, the weather had come up trumps, too.

Kate turned from the window and made her slow way across the room to get herself a cup of tea. Prayer always worked, she reminded herself.

The good Lord never quite forgot her. True, things didn't always work out the way she hoped.

Prayer hadn't saved her sight on that day last year when the doctors had told her she'd never see again.

But, instead, it had brought her to this safe little room, in sheltered housing, with a kind warden, and friendly neighbours.

Prayer hadn't brought her marriage or children, either; but it had brought her Norah, dear Arthur's grandchild, who was coming today.

Norah, the beloved great-niece who always seemed to understand her.

I've got a lot to be thankful for, Kate told herself, listening for the whistle of the kettle that would signal the water was boiling.

Her fingers groped along the kitchen shelf for the familiar cup and saucer, in their familiar places. She could manage quite well in this room of hers, with the help of Mrs Lane, the warden.

Kind Mrs Lane, who had been almost as excited as herself when she had heard about the trip to the country.

That would be her now, tapping on the door, on her rounds of the residents.

★ ★ ★ ★

Kate, sipping her tea, raised a beaming face as she heard the door click open. "Would you believe it, Mrs Lane! After last night's downpour! So incredible."

"It's going to be a glorious day."

The warden sat down in a chair. "You're right, Miss Bentley. Your luck's in today."

"It is indeed," Kate said. "Well, I think I've got everything ready."

Her blurred eyes searched about the room. "Coat, hat, gloves — mustn't go out without gloves — handbag. I don't want to waste a minute when Norah arrives."

"Of course you don't." Mrs Lane smiled. "Now, we've packed you some sandwiches and a flask of coffee.

"It's lucky your Norah was able to come south, since she lives so far away.

"She's having a college interview, did you say?"

Kate nodded. "She's a bright enough lass." She remembered the fresh young voice over the phone.

"Aunt Kate, can I take you for a day in the country? You'll never believe it but I've a college interview quite near your place and the folks are lending me their car.

"Mum says I can stay over Sunday somewhere and, when I told Grandad, he said I should look you up and give you a run out.

"You'd like that, wouldn't you?" Norah had asked tentatively.

Like it! To Kate, it had seemed like a miracle.

"And where do you plan to go?" Mrs Lane was asking.

Kate pressed her fingers together in her lap. "There's one place above all I want to visit, Mrs Lane. Elbury."

The Warden hesitated. "Elbury? Well, it's quite a way."

"But not too far," Kate said confidently. "Norah said so."

"Well, I don't suppose it is for young folk used to charging around in a car."

"It's where I grew up," Kate explained.

"But — supposing it's changed? You might not feel the same way."

"It can't have changed," Kate said with confidence.

"Little places like Elbury don't.

"It's a perfect little village," Kate went on.

"My brother, Arthur — Norah's grandfather — and I had such happy times there.

"I've never been back. All my life I've promised myself . . . but there, you won't want to hear about that.

"I just can't believe I'm really going there."

Kate paused, anxious not to tempt fate. "That is, if Norah can still take me."

"You're sure you *want* to go?"

Kate nodded. "I may not be able to see, but I can sit on the bench on Elbury Hill and look down on the village. I know every stick and stone of it, you see.

"I can feel the sun on my face and the fresh wind — there's always a fresh wind up there, Mrs Lane, however hot it is in the valley.

"And great skies with wonderful passing clouds. I may not see the clouds but I can still hear the larks singing.

"There's no better place in the world than Elbury Hill to hear the larks singing."

She broke off, hearing the scrunch of tyres on gravel outside, the sharp slam of a car door.

"She's here!" Kate cried, and struggled from her chair.

✱   ✱   ✱   ✱

"We must be pretty near now," Norah said.

It was good to be sitting here in Norah's little car, Kate thought, hearing the young voice by her side.

Good to have the whole day to herself; to be going where she wanted to go. Cars made such a difference; they ate up the miles.

Norah had thought nothing of finding her way to a strange place with a map.

And already they'd passed one signpost for Elbury.

The next one, Kate told herself, should say Elbury Hill. Round a corner, up a long, winding road, turn to the left, the bend and then . . .

"It's uphill all the way now, Aunt Kate," Norah said. "Quite a climb. Just fields each side, that's all."

"And the hedges!" Kate said. "Hedges full of meadowsweet.

"This time of year they were always beautiful."

"Now we're coming to a bend — left, did you say?" Norah broke in on Kate's happy chatter.

"Left," Kate echoed.

"Soon you'll see a clump of trees, right on the horizon. Elms, they are, with great spreading branches. Lovely trees, elms — you watch out for them, dear.

"And, on the further side, there's a bench. With a view."

Norah was silent as the little car climbed upward, concentrating on her driving, Kate suspected.

"A clump of elms," Kate repeated almost to herself. "You can't miss them. Right on the skyline. Like sentinels, we always said, Arthur and I.

"Everyone knows the Elbury elms."

Norah slowed the car. "There's been a clump of trees here; yes, I can see that.

"But, not now. They've been cut down."

Kate caught her breath. "Not my elms?"

"I'm afraid so, Aunt Kate. Don't you remember? Dutch elm disease."

Kate's fingers twisted in her lap. "Oh, Norah! My elms! Why, we used to bring picnics up here when it was hot in the valley.

"It was always cool under those elms. You could lie under the branches and look up at the sky.

"They were beautiful trees!"

Norah laid a light hand on her aunt's arm. "Never mind, Aunt Kate. There's the hilltop. I'm dying to see this view you've told me so much about."

The car began to bump and Kate knew they had left the road and were crossing the track.

Up there, there was a seat, overlooking the valley. They must be nearly at it.

"Just you wait, Norah dear," Kate said proudly.

"Wait till you see that view!"

Norah brought the car to a halt and gently helped Kate out.

The old lady felt the wind fresh on her cheek and raised her face to the sky, a little giddy from excitement, glad of Norah's arm.

High above the larks were singing.

"It's just the same!" Kate breathed excitedly. "Oh, I can feel it's just the same!"

She let the girl lead her to the bench on the brow of the hill.

Running gnarled fingers over the wood, she knew it was a different seat.

The old bench had been rough; this one was smooth and shiny. But it was in the same place, after all.

How often had she and Arthur sat here, looking out over Elbury.

Her brother had known all the landmarks.

Now, it was the turn of Arthur's grandchild to point them out.

K ATE sat back comfortably and searched for the girl's hand. "Well, dear," she said, "and what do you think of Elbury?" She heard the catch of breath. It always took people like that, she remembered. The view was magnificent, everyone said. She squeezed Norah's hand. "I knew you'd find it beautiful."

Norah did not speak.

"The best view in the county," Kate prompted.

Norah seemed to be fumbling with her handbag; what was the dear child doing? Kate waited.

And then Norah found her voice. "It's — it's really beautiful," Norah said slowly.

Kate laughed softly. "I thought you'd say that. All that stretch of green countryside and, below, the church amongst the trees.

"They haven't cut down those elms by the church, have they?"

Sudden fear gripped her. "Don't say they've cut down those as well!"

Norah's words came slowly. "No, Aunt Kate. Don't worry. Your elms are there, down in the valley — all round the church, like you said.

"And the tower rising up from them is of beautiful grey stone."

"It's a wonderful view."

Kate sighed happily. "That's where the rooks build. Arthur and I used to count the nests on Sundays as we walked to church.

"And, on summer evenings, you'd see them all flying home to those elms — and what a noise they made! Pity we aren't here tonight to listen to their cawing.

"What else can you see, dear? The school by the church? That hasn't changed, has it? A little grey school, like the church tower — with high windows and a belfry.

"See it?"

Norah's voice was even. "Yes, Aunt Kate. There's the school. And the belfry."

"I don't suppose the old school bell still hangs there?" Kate said dreamily. "Arthur and I used to run like mad when that bell stopped ringing.

"They'll have taken that away, perhaps?"

"No," Norah said. "I can still see the school bell. It's not easy, but I can just make it out.

"And the schoolyard, too. By the church wall."

Kate leaned back, her face thoughtful. "I'm glad that hasn't changed, dear.

"That wall was where the girls used to sit when the boys were bowling their iron hoops in the yard. They'd bowl at our legs, just for devilment. So we sat up there out of harm's way.

"Many's a time I've dangled my feet from the top of that wall.

"Is the school house still there? Next to the yard, on the right?

"Old Mr Hughes was our schoolmaster then. A white house with gables; see it?"

"Gables." Norah paused. "Yes, I see it."

"And the shop, a bit further on? You can't see our cottage from here; that was behind the church; but the shop you could see.

"Ted Turner's shop, where they sold everything — sweets, groceries, candles and boots.

"Arthur and I used to run there for our Saturday sweets; liquorice for him, jelly babies for me.

"And, sometimes, old Ted used to let me go up on a wooden box till I was high enough to reach the bacon slicer.

"I'd stand up there watching the slices fall as I turned the handle."

She sighed. "You don't get bacon sliced like that any more; it's all this ready-wrapped stuff."

"Yes," Norah said slowly. "Yes, there's the shop."

Kate was silent a moment; then turned her head the other way. "The river can't have changed," she said happily.

"Down at the end of the street, running between high banks, with a sandy stretch in the middle.

"There's a wooden bridge where you cross; maybe the bridge is different now, is it?"

Norah paused. "There's your wooden bridge, Aunt Kate. Just the same."

"We used to lean over the bridge and watch for tiddlers," Kate said.

"And, once, Arthur got into a fight with some boys and was pushed in.

"He came home all dripping, and I had to plead with Mother not to be cross. Remind your grandad about that when you get home, won't you?"

"I will," Norah said. "I'll have a lot to tell him."

Kate felt the girl's hand slip suddenly into hers, warm and reassuring. "Happy, Aunt Kate?" she asked.

"Very happy," Kate murmured.

The sun was making her drowsy. Or was it all that driving?

Rides into the country did tend to make you sleepy. She'd just close her eyes for a moment and rest — and remember.

It was Norah's voice that woke her. Time was getting on.

"We ought to be going, Aunt Kate."

Kate shook herself. "You should have wakened me, child.

"There won't be time to go down into the village now."

"Did you really want to?" Norah asked.

Kate considered. Going down to the village would mean bustle and movement; and Norah guiding her. She would have to watch her step and no-one down there would remember her.

Perhaps it was best to leave things as they were; this seat in the sunshine, and the view from Elbury Hill.

"I think we'll go back," she announced.

Did you enjoy your day, Miss Bentley?" the warden, Mrs Lane, asked. It had been a long drive home; the sun was already low in the sky, and shadows lay across the grass. Norah, shepherding her aunt from the car, smiled across at Mrs Lane. "I think she did."

"Oh, it was perfect!" Kate said, clasping her hands.

"Absolutely perfect. All just as it used to be. An answer to my prayer."

"That's lovely," the warden said cheerfully. "But you must be feeling a bit thirsty now. There's some tea in the dining-room, Miss Bentley, if you'd like to go on ahead."

THE warden and the young woman watched the stocky little figure making her way confidently to the dining-room. She knew the way so well. "I'm so glad the visit didn't disappoint her," the warden said softly. "I was a bit worried the place would have changed."

There was silence, then Norah sighed.

"So was I, and I'm afraid it had. All the trees — those lovely elms have gone and the school's a modern place of glass and concrete.

"The schoolhouse is now a modern villa; and the shop, a supermarket.

"There's still the river, of course, but the wooden bridge has been replaced by a huge metal invention that lorries speed over. If it hadn't been Sunday, she'd have heard them.

"The place has changed out of all recognition. But, at least, she'll never know."

The girl hesitated.

"But I don't understand, Norah. She seemed so happy!"

"That's why I did it, Mrs Lane."

"Did it? Did what, my dear?"

The girl fumbled in her handbag and drew out a faded picture postcard.

"That was Elbury," she whispered.

The warden took it and turned it over in her hand.

"Grandad gave it to me to bring to Aunt Kate," Norah said.

"He knew where I was taking her and he thought she'd like to show her friends here where she was visiting.

"But I don't know — maybe he guessed . . ."

Mrs Lane stepped back. "You mean — this is what you described to her?"

Norah nodded. "I'm afraid so. You don't think I did wrong?"

Mrs Lane tucked the postcard back again into Norah's bag and laid a hand on her shoulder.

"No, I don't. It was the kindest thing to do."

"This way," Norah murmured, as they walked on into the house, "Aunt Kate will be able to keep her view from the hill for ever." ∎

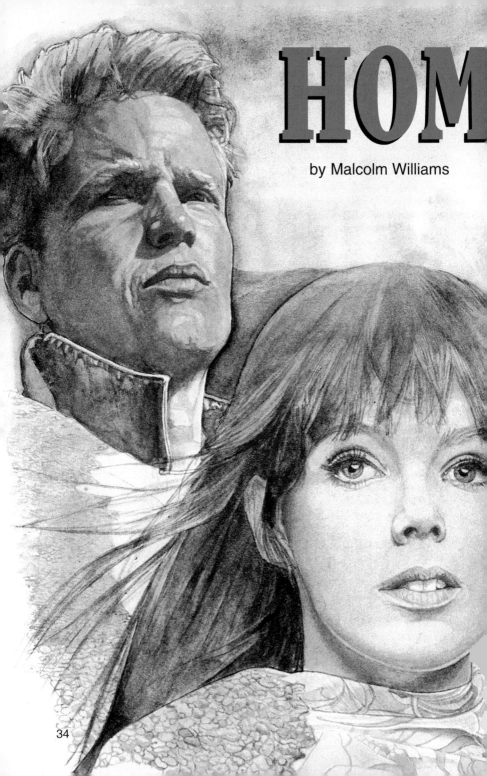

HOM

by Malcolm Williams

ECOMING

They'd all made a mistake so many years ago — now he had to make sure his daughter wasn't the one who paid for it.

MARTIN PARRISH turned up his raincoat collar as he stood beneath the dripping lime tree, watching the big house. The rain was pecking gently at the leaves and an amber street lamp cast a soft puddle of light over the pavement.

The house itself looked forlorn. The paintwork was peeling badly, the front garden was overgrown. Even the large sign spelling out: "Roy And Susan Grey — Academy Of Dancing" was in need of renovation — and correction. It should only read "Susan Grey" now.

The building was in darkness, except for a single light burning upstairs. Martin wondered why, then remembered that Sunday had always been the day of rest at the school. The remainder of the week was filled with lessons: ballet, tap, modern, ballroom, Latin-American . . .

At least, that's how it used to be, Martin recalled. Now he didn't know what went on inside those three spacious studios.

He'd been standing here in the shadows for quarter of an hour and after eight years in Australia the chill dampness of the English spring was beginning to unnerve him. He stamped his feet.

I should go back to the hotel, he thought. Forget about the house — the academy. Just walk away.

But he couldn't.

Instead, he pulled his collar even higher against the cold.

Once, long ago, he'd been told never to come back here again. It had been the night he'd told the Greys he was going to marry their daughter, Lois, and take her away with him to Melbourne.

And seven years ago, when Lois had died giving birth to his daughter, Susy, he'd assumed he never would return.

Thinking of his daughter, now asleep in the hotel bedroom, filled him with a familiar, almost overwhelming sense of protectiveness. He hadn't wanted to leave her even for half an hour, while he went out for this walk. But he couldn't bring her with him, so, in the end, he'd asked the hotel owner's wife to keep an eye on her.

"Where are you going, Daddy?" Susy had asked curiously.

"For some fresh air, love. And there's someone I want to see."

She'd accepted his answer without question, as always.

Now, in the shadows of the park, Martin walked as far as the small wooden bower where he and Lois used to go after his lessons. But he didn't enter.

Conscious that it would revive too many memories — of long, summer nights . . . of wintry, starry skies . . . of he and Lois shivering and holding hands in the moonlight — he walked past.

Martin grimaced and turned back, suddenly realising how wrong it was to have come. He was trembling now, not just with the cold, but with his memories — memories of that first time he'd rung the bell at the academy to enrol for a crash course in ballroom dancing.

M Y problem is simple," Martin had told Susan Grey frankly. "I have two left feet." "We can cure that!" she had assured him breezily. "How about private lessons?" "I only want to learn the rudiments," he'd said hesitantly. "To stop me making a fool of myself at dances."

The overseas posting had been in the offing at the time and he'd known there would be a round of social occasions when he got there.

What he hadn't known was that the dancing lessons would lead to him falling in love with his dancing teacher. It was Lois, vivacious and vital, who had been his tutor.

Lois had been trained "at considerable expense" to work at her parents' academy, to take over when her parents retired. Her mother had planned it all. What she hadn't planned on was Lois becoming involved with one of the customers, before her dreams came true.

It was when she'd found out about their little meetings in the park that the rows had started. He'd had to end the classes, but they'd still met. The fact that their dates were secret and forbidden only made them more precious.

Then — one dark, starry night in October — they'd decided to get married immediately . . .

Lois had told her parents straightaway. A loving daughter, she had wanted to include them in her happiness.

Horrified, they'd tried to dissuade her. And the more they'd tried, the more determined Lois had become . . . Until, without her parents' consent, she had quietly married him.

It wasn't until after the wedding that Lois had told her parents she was carrying Martin's child.

Any hopes of parental blessing had died there.

Before leaving Britain, Martin had seen Lois's parents only once more. Her mother had done most of the talking and when, angry and hurt, she'd accused Martin of stealing her daughter away from her, Martin knew he and Lois had been "cast off".

In her few, short months in Australia, Lois had written home often, but her letters had gone unanswered. She never really got over that. Even in the happiness of her pregnancy, there was always a touch of sadness.

And then, tragically, she'd died.

Her last wish had been to christen their daughter "Susan", after her mother . . .

Bitterness had soured Martin at first. He'd respected Lois's wishes but, though the time after her death was an unending nightmare, he had kept the grief private. He had never even contacted her parents after that one, brief letter about their daughter's death.

Somehow, his love and responsibility towards his little girl had enabled him to survive his loss. And now he'd returned to England, to a post up north that would give him more time to devote himself to Susy.

★   ★   ★   ★

The rain began to fall heavily now. Already, there were dark patches on the shoulders of his raincoat. Even so, Martin stood there for a while.

Staring sightlessly at his feet, he marvelled at the coincidence that had happened two days ago, when he'd first arrived back. He had bumped into an old friend, Ben Harwich. It had been Ben who'd told Martin about Roy Grey's death.

"I don't want to put a damper on things, Martin," he'd said. "But you obviously don't know . . . Your father-in-law had a stroke three weeks ago. I'm sorry. He never recovered."

Martin's head jerked up as the rain strummed down on the park. Father-in-law, mother-in-law . . .? He'd never been able to think of them that way.

So what had prompted him to break his journey — come back to the place where he'd decided never to return?

Since leaving the hotel, he'd wondered about that. Standing in the shadows, watching the house, he thought deeply on it again. Could it be conscience, after all these years? Because she was lonely, as he had been, even though he had Susy.

He shook his head. No, this wasn't the way. He shouldn't have come back here alone. It would only re-open old wounds.

Thrusting his hands deeply into his pockets, Martin trudged back across the park — away from the house, towards his hotel . . .

ON Monday morning, Susan Grey came downstairs, carefully dressed and made-up, ready to battle with another empty day. Automatically, she unlocked the big front door of the dancing academy, picking up the mail and the milk bottles. In half an hour's time, her first dancing class was scheduled to start and she was thankful for that. It kept her occupied, pulled her through the day.

She paused on the top front step to check the weather. Across the street, the giant lime tree was still dripping gently. But it had stopped raining.

She went inside, checked the top studio, prepared the tapes for the morning's music.

Pausing to glance at herself in the hall mirror she saw a face lined by toil, grief — and seven long years of self-recrimination. *Oh, Roy . . .*

But it was too late now for any more tears — always too late. All she could do was mask her pain from the world. She was just applying an extra touch of eye shadow when the front doorbell rang. Strange, she wasn't expecting anyone yet.

Slowly, Susan went to the door, consciously adjusting her expression to a professional smile of welcome.

"Good morning. Can I help you?"

The little girl looking innocently up at her might have been any one of the scores of children who came for ballet lessons at the school. But Susan felt her hard-won calm begin to slip. There was something about the child . . .

Susan smiled again and looked up at the man holding the girl's hand.

He hesitated, then said: "I'd like to enrol my daughter for a course of ballet lessons. Her mother would have — I would like her to learn."

"Martin?" Susan whispered, unaware she had taken a step forward.

There was a pause, then: "And this —?"

"My name is Susy," the little girl told her. "Susy Parrish."

Susan gazed down, too overwhelmed to speak. Then she bent and put her hands on the girl's shoulders.

"Well, Susy Parrish," she murmured. "You and your daddy are very, very welcome." ■

It wasn't easy convincing her he was a true hero. Especially when he was the one in distress!

by Sarah Burkhill

HER KNIGHT IN SHINING APRON

GARY, would you like a lobster?" That's my mother for you! Anyone else starts off a telephone conversation by enquiring about your health or something. But not my mum. She believes in getting straight to the point.

As the phone call came at eight o'clock on a Saturday morning and awakened me from a deep sleep, I had a little difficulty in grasping that point!

"What?" I mumbled vaguely, grabbing at the top of my pyjama trousers, before they could descend further.

"A lobster," she repeated impatiently. "I ordered one from the fishmonger for your dad and me to have a celebration meal for our wedding anniversary . . ."

Clang! I'd forgotten about that.

"Oh, yes. Happy anniversary. I'll be bringing your present round —" I began hastily, but the purpose of the call had not been to jog my failing memory, and she babbled on.

". . . And *then,* Dad announced this morning that he was taking me away for the weekend as a surprise . . ."

"Very nice. Have a good —"

". . . *So,* would you like the lobster?" she continued. "It's paid for and it seems a shame to waste it.

"You'd just have to collect it from McMillan's, the fish shop in High Street. You know, opposite the bank?"

The mention of banks reminded me of the current state of my finances, a state that bodied ill for my impending dinner date with Lorraine Shaw.

The lobster, suddenly, was the answer to a young man's prayers.

"Great," I said, my mind racing.

A romantic dinner here at the flat. Cold lobster and salad and a decanted bottle of supermarket plonk.

Candles on the table to create the right atmosphere and also to disguise the state of the room — and Lorraine smiling in Mona-Lisa fashion from across the table.

So, it hardly compared with being taken to the Ritz!

But, it was still a darn sight better than that Italian place at Weston, and a plate of half-boiled string with lumpy tomato paste squirted over it.

And, more to the point, with a free lobster it was also cheaper.

'D been seeing Lorraine for about four weeks, which accounted for my impecunious state. I suppose it was just showing off on my part but, then, I'd never had anyone like Lorraine to show off to before. Lorraine was *special.*

Lorraine was the kind of girl I'd dreamed about for the better half of my 24 years, and I had been on an all-out drive to impress her.

I gave her a quick phone call to suggest I cook dinner at the flat, instead of going out for a meal, then endeavoured to clean the place up a bit.

Then, by 11.30 a.m., I had set off for McMillan's to collect my lobster.

"It's the one ordered for Mrs Mitchell," I told the man, adding hastily, "and it's paid for."

As he went through to the back, I considered what I might do with the thing once I got it home.

My cooking wasn't too bad, on the whole, but I had never actually tackled a lobster before.

"How do you cook them?" I asked, when he reappeared in the front shop.

"Depends what you want," he replied. "You could have lobster thermidor, lobster Parisienne, lobster —"

"I just want plain, ordinary lobster with some salad stuff," I interrupted firmly.

My cooking wasn't *that* good.

"In that case, just drop it into boiling water and boil for about ten minutes for every pound. By then it will have turned red. Leave it to cool.

"Then it's quite easy to serve. Just open it up down the centre and cut here and here —"

He was pointing to indicate where the incisions should be, but broke off when he saw the expression on my face.

"It's moving!" I said in horror. "It's alive!"

A tiny bell rang somewhere at the back of my mind.

Had I once heard a horrific-sounding account of how lobsters were cooked?

If so, I had chosen to forget it immediately.

"Well, of course it's alive," he said witheringly. "It's supposed to be."

He placed the lobster in my carrier, on top of the lettuce, tomatoes and half cucumber I'd got down the road.

"And don't worry about it nipping you. Its claws are tied, so it's perfectly harmless!"

That was worse. This monster was suggesting I boil alive a perfectly-harmless little lobster!

"Have you never cooked one before, son?" an old lady who had come in after me inquired.

"Did you not know they were cooked alive?"

She smiled benignly. "There's nothing to it, really.

"Sometimes it makes a bit of a noise at first and some people think that's the poor thing screaming. But it's only the fact that there's air escaping."

Before I could say anything, she had turned to the fishmonger and asked for a couple of pounds of herring, so I had no option but to move off, bearing the lobster with me.

A T home, I was no more enthusiastic about the situation. Why did it always happen to *me?* Anybody else's mother would have ordered a nice, middle cut of salmon for their anniversary dinner. Or a turkey, perhaps, all trussed up and decently dead.

But, not mine. Oh, no.

Mine's got to land me with a real, living-and-breathing lobster, thereby turning her only son into a murderer overnight.

I tipped it out onto a work surface. It was a pretty ugly-looking brute but, then, I'm no oil painting myself. That doesn't give people the right to go around boiling me alive.

Still, it would have to be done.

"Sorry, old pal," I told the ill-fated crustacean.

"But, as Lorraine is coming to dinner and the only edible things in the place are you and a packet of sausages, I'm afraid I've no choice."

I filled a large saucepan with water and set it on the cooker, wishing there was a kinder way of going about it.

On the work surface, the lobster was flexing its claws at me and edging its way slowly across the surface.

Gingerly I pushed it into the sink with a wooden spoon before it built up speed and escaped altogether, then I turned my back on it and waited for the water to boil.

"It'll be very quick," I assured my victim, suspending it over the bubbling water. "It'll only take —"

Good question. How long *would* it take? Two seconds? Ten? Thirty? A minute?

The lobster waved a tethered claw in a gesture which could have been interpreted as either threatening or imploring.

I chose to take it as the latter and, with a despairing sigh, returned him to the sink.

It was no use. Kind-hearted, sensitive, gentle people like me were never designed to be murderers.

It would take someone with a much stronger stomach; someone with a cruel and uncaring nature and the ability to disregard totally the suffering that might be inflicted on a fellow creature.

It would take, in short, a woman . . .!

"Um — Madge — I'm having a bit of a problem," I said pathetically to the woman upstairs.

"Do you think you could come down for a minute and give me a hand?"

She's a good sort, is Madge. She's helped me out on several occasions with unpleasant things — like removing spiders from the bath and opening recalcitrant tins of corned beef.

She gazed into the sink at my lobster, temporarily reprieved and exploring its exciting new surroundings.

"But why did you buy it?" she asked. "Didn't you know lobsters were supposed to be cooked alive?"

If anyone else said that, I promised myself, I'd thump them.

"Well, I suppose I did know, somewhere in the dim, dark recesses of my mind," I told her hesitantly.

"But I forgot.

"I mean, you don't go around constantly worrying about lobsters, do you?

"And, anyway," I finished lamely. "I didn't buy it. It was a present."

Madge shot me an odd look which showed her opinion of anyone who gave live lobsters as presents, but I didn't bother to explain.

"So, if you could just put him in the pot for me, I'd be much obliged," I said instead.

Made wasn't being her usual helpful self.

"I don't see why you can't do it yourself," she reproved.

"Honestly, Gary, you can be an awful wimp at times!

"Just pick him — it," she corrected, "up and drop it in."

"I can't!" I cringed.

"Go on, Madge, please. Do it for me. I'll give you a bit later if you do it for me.

"There's too much there for just Lorraine and me."

She cast an eye over the captive.

"I quite like lobster," she volunteered.

"But I usually buy them ready cooked. I've never actually — well — *done* one, as it were."

"You don't want to do it, do you?" I accused. "You're scared of it."

"No I'm not. I just — well — don't feel very comfortable about it.

"In fact," she admitted, "the very idea of dropping something that's alive into boiling water . . ."

She shuddered. "No, sorry, Gary, but you're on your own this time."

The bell rang and I went to answer the door. It was a man collecting for medical research. I dragged him in.

"Do you know anything about lobsters?"

"Lobsters?"

He looked a bit taken aback at suddenly finding himself removed from the doorstep and placed in my kitchen, but he didn't protest.

"Well —" He scratched his head. "They're crustaceans, edible crustaceans, with large strong claws."

He broke off and pointed. "That's one, there."

"Yes, I know it is," I told him patiently.

"But I don't want it there. I want it in that pot of boiling water.

"Could you put it in for me?"

"Me?"

"Uh-huh. I'll give you a pound if you put it in for me."

He looked tempted for a moment, then peered closer at the lobster.

"Well,, I don't think . . . I mean, I've never actually . . .

"No," he said firmly, if regretfully. "No, my wife could do it if she were here, but I really don't think I could.

"It's — well — it seems cruel, doesn't it?"

Madge and I nodded.

"That's the trouble," I admitted. "Neither of us can quite bring ourself to do it."

THE three of us stared disconsolately at the lobster. Its malevolent eye stared back. The charity man brightened suddenly. "Couldn't we kill it first? Kill it humanely, I mean, and then put it in?" "We could gas it," Madge said excitedly. "We could put it in the oven and gas it! That'd be painless."

"Wouldn't work," I pointed out. "It's non-poisonous gas now, isn't it? We'd just blow the thing up and ourselves with it."

Back to the drawing board.

43

"We could bash its head in with a mallet," the man suggested.

I winced. "That doesn't sound very humane to me."

"Well, it's better than getting boiled alive, isn't it?"

I supposed that were true.

"OK." I agreed. "You do it then."

"*Me?*" He looked horrified.

"Not on your life. It's your lobster. *You* bash its head in."

His expression changed from one of horror to one of irritation, and he shook his collecting can at me.

"Look, are you going to contribute or not? 'Cause, if you're not, stop wasting my time and let me get on to people who will."

With a bad grace, I shoved a coin in his can, and he decamped.

"Fat lot of good he was," I complained.

"Yes, and a fat lot of good I am, too, I'm afraid," Madge said.

"I'm sorry, love, but I'll have to get back upstairs."

"We're going to my sister's tonight and I've still to wash my hair."

Thus saying, Madge abandoned me, too, and I was left alone with the lobster.

I glanced at the clock. Lorraine would be here in just under four hours.

If it was to be cooked in time for dinner, the deed would have to be done now.

"Right, chum!" I addressed him forcefully. "Like it or not, your number's up!"

* * * *

Though I say so myself, the dinner table was a work of art.

To make up for failing to help with the lobster, Madge had lent me her crystal wine glasses and best china.

For a centrepiece, I had bought some flowers from a nearby florist.

Two red candles cast a gentle glow over everything and made Lorraine look almost ethereal as she sat opposite me.

"That was a very nice meal, Gary," she told me, flashing that Mona-Lisa smile.

I shrugged in embarrassment.

"It's very kind of you to say so but it wasn't really, was it?" I said miserably, staring down at the plate of plain biscuits I'd heaped together as dessert.

"Oh, but it was," she insisted.

"I mean it. I'm very partial to sausages. And they were beautifully cooked."

She got up. "Now, you must let me do the washing up for you," she went on, gathering up the plates.

"No, just leave them. I'll do them in the morning.

"Just go back through and sit down," I finished.

Her face was a study.

44

"Gary," she said slowly, "do you know you've got a lobster in your sink?"

Hanging my head, I told her the whole story and waited for her to start laughing at me.

Much to my surprise, she didn't.

"But — but what you are going to do with it?" she asked.

"You can't just leave it there. It'll die anyway in a few hours."

"Well, then — maybe after it's died of — um — natural causes, as it were — maybe then I could cook it, and we could go to the coast tomorrow and have a picnic?"

Lorraine shook her head.

"I've got a better idea," she suggested. "Let's go to the coast now . . ."

It was a beautiful night. We sat on a flat rock, looking out over the still, moon-lit water and Lorraine laid her head on my shoulder.

"I think I'm falling in love with you a little," she said slowly.

"Before tonight, I tended to be a bit wary of you.

"You always seemed so confident, in control and sure of yourself.

"You made me feel I had to be on my best behaviour all the time."

She kissed my nose. "But, now I know you're just a silly old softy at heart."

"I was a bit frightened of you, too," I admitted.

"You always seemed so cool, aloof and perfect.

"I couldn't imagine what you saw in me and I was afraid you'd get fed up."

She gave me a quick, reassuring hug, then looked back out to sea. "Do you think he'll be all right?"

"Well, he seemed to be. He looked a bit stunned at first when he got back in the water. But he took off fast enough afterwards, didn't he?"

I examined my finger, round which Lorraine had wrapped a paper hankie.

"I must say he could have shown a bit more gratitude when I cut the ties on his claws."

The blood was still oozing out of the wound and she took the tissue and dabbed at it gently.

"It's after midnight," I said reluctantly. "I suppose I really ought to be taking you home."

"Later," she said, turning to me.

★　★　★　★

". . . And then, we went to a show at night," my mother finished enthusiastically.

"I'm glad you had a good time," I said into the phone. "And I *will* be bringing your present round soon . . ."

"How did the lobster go?" she asked.

"Swimmingly!" I told her. ∎

THE SWANS

by Joyce Stranger

Inspired by an illustration by Mark Viney

Spring.
New life comes to the river.
In her hidden holt the she otter guards her cubs
So small and helpless.
When four weeks old she takes them into the open spaces
And teaches them to love and trust the water.
The world around them is a source of wonder.
They learn that the wind shakes the trees and rustles in the rushes.
They see ducks diving.
They see swallows dipping after flies almost skimming the wave tops.
They see creamy ruffles on the bue water, hear frogs croaking
And listen to the soft gurgling trill of distant curlews.
Then, one day, they see a wonder
As the Queen of the river
The long necked swan, her feathers purest white
Glides past them, seeming part of the rippling water.
She lifts her wings, bends her neck, and her six downy cygnets swim behind her
Grey and soft among the yellow irises.
Beyond them is her consort, watchful, guarding
Aware of hawk and crow in the air
And the wicked pike with his death-dealing teeth
And his giant appetite, lying beneath the tranquil surface.
The cob threatens, ready to drive all danger from his young family.
His mate floats towards her nest, serene and elegant.
When night darkens the world she sleeps
Her cygnets safe beneath her, sheltered by her encircling wings.
Her mate patrols the water, hisses at the curious otter cubs
Who dive for shelter, hiding deep in the holt.
They too sleep while the great swan dominates the river,
Ready to drive off the many dangers that threaten his young.
Faithful for ever he stands watch, silvered by moonlight.
A passing fisherman pauses, savouring his beauty.

BEDTIME STORY

Of course he believed in fairy tales. Once upon a time, he'd even believed in happy endings . . .

by Sarah Burkhill

TOM turned his key in the door, stepped into the hallway and tripped over a doll's pram. "Mummy? Mum-*eee*!" his daughter's voice issued urgently from upstairs. "Mum-ee, I'm ready!" A basket of laundry folded for ironing sat at the open kitchen door, and from the living-room he could hear baby Alistair screaming loudly.

So it had been one of *those* days, had it? Tom sighed. Sally would be in a mood again, and it would not be improved by his late homecoming.

He hung his raincoat on the hall stand and braced himself.

"Hi! I got held up on a call over at Millburn."

Sally was trying to rub some ointment into Alistair's gums. Alistair, his face contorted with rage, wasn't having any.

"Mummy?" Heather called again.

"Your chop's in the frying pan. Heat it up," Sally said, not even bothering to look at him. "And you'll just have to fry up the potatoes along with it."

Tom watched her for a moment.

"Yeah. Sure." He turned away, wishing he'd taken Chris Campbell up on that offer of a pint.

He could have had a microwaved spaghetti bolognaise at the pub, in pleasant surroundings and in the company of boozily-cheerful people.

Tom had had a bad day, too. There had been a lot of them recently, and bad nights as well he could do without.

"Mum-eeee!" Heather was nothing if not persistent.

"Oh, for goodness' sake see what she wants!" Sally said irritably. "She'll wake Iain up and he's only just asleep!"

His five-year-old was sitting up in bed, surrounded by a pile of books and wearing a peeved and impatient expression.

It changed to a conspiratorial smile when she saw him.

"You're late! Mummy was angry. She threw your vegetables out, 'cause she said they wouldn't heat up.

"Did you go for a drink?" she continued artlessly. "Mummy said she bet you'd gone for a drink."

"Well I didn't." Tom ruffled her hair. "What were you calling for? Your mum's busy with the baby."

Heather screwed her face up. "She's *always* busy with Alistair. He's a terrible baby. He's even worse than Iain was."

"You can't remember Iain as a baby."

"Can!"

Tom knew better than to argue.

"So what did you want?"

Heather gave a long-suffering sigh. "Mummy was *supposed* to come and read me a story. She said she'd come before I went to sleep, and if she doesn't hurry up I'll *be* asleep, 'cause I'm tired tonight."

Tom thought about his reheated chop and potatoes, and sat down on the edge of the bed. They could wait.

"Well, I'll read to you instead. Which story do you want?"

"This one." Heather held up a book open about halfway through. "The one about the lonely princess, who lives in a great big huge castle on the edge of —"

"Who's telling this story, you or me?" Tom grinned at her.

"You are." She sat back on her pillows and returned the grin.

O NCE upon a time," he started, "there was a beautiful princess. She lived in a land called —" "What did she look like?" Heather interrupted. Tom flipped the page over in search of an illustration, but for this particular story there wasn't one.

"What did she *look* like?" Heather repeated.

"Oh, like — just like you," he said.

His daughter shot him a look of reprimand.

"She couldn't have. She couldn't, 'cause she's a lady and I'm only a little girl."

"Well — like your mum, then," he amended, and Heather giggled.

"Mum doesn't look like a princess!"

No, more like the wicked witch. He pictured her as he'd come in tonight, her hair pushed roughly behind her ears and a strained, tight expression on her face as she'd snapped at him. Then he shrugged away the uncharitable thought.

"She used to, though," he told his daughter. "When I knew her at first, she looked exactly like a princess.

"She had glossy chestnut hair that hung down to her shoulders, and big, shining eyes that always seemed to be laughing."

Heather looked a bit sceptical.

"And were you the handsome prince?" she asked.

"Yes," Tom said firmly. "Look, madam, do you want this story or don't you?"

Heather nodded vigorously and he continued. "She lived in a land called Fantasia, that was right on the very edge of the world, and one day, while she was . . ."

TOM read on, but his mind wasn't on the words printed before him. Instead, it dwelt on those Sally had said to him last night, *Said,* not shrieked. It wasn't a row as such. They didn't have rows now. Sometimes, in the once-upon-a-time days, he had almost looked forward to the occasional fall-out he and Sally would have — because the making up would be so wonderful.

But not these days. Rows were too positive. These days they just seemed to chip away at each other, like a sculptor with a chisel.

Last night's episode had started in the usual way. He'd come in at six, had a meal, helped settled Iain, then sank back in a chair to watch the film that started at 7.15.

"You were going to drill a hole in the kitchen so's the food mixer could be hung up," she said at the first commercial break.

"This week, I said. *Sometime* this week. Not necessarily tonight."

"Oh, it never is! You're always putting things off."

"Look, I've had a busy day. Johnson was up from head office. Tonight I want to sit and relax. OK?"

She had got up and ostentatiously started to clean the insides of the window.

The inference was clear. *I've had a busy day, too, but I've still got work to do.*

"Oh, for goodness' sake!" He had got up and snapped off the television. "OK. Where's it to go?"

"Don't bother." She polished the window harder. "It'll probably just fall down again anyway if you put it up. The last thing you put up fell down again."

Tom had stared at her.

Once, you used to make me feel 10 feet tall, he thought.

Her eyes — the beautiful, sparkling eyes he had just described to Heather — had been irritable and accusing as she'd looked back at him.

Once, you used to be 10 feet tall, they seemed to say to him.

"Daddy!"

Tom glanced up from the book to find his daughter frowning at him.

"You've stopped. You've stopped reading and it isn't the end yet.

"It can't be the end, 'cause we haven't had the happy ever after."

"Sorry, chicken. Where were we?"

"Her father wouldn't let her marry the prince, because he was poor."

Tom started to read again.

Happy ever after. That's the way he'd thought it would be, that day he and Sally were married at the little parish church of St Oswald's.

She had been so beautiful that day, like something out of a fairy-tale in her flowing white dress. His Sally.

It had been a late afternoon wedding, and after the ceremony they'd had a reception at the Golden Fleece Hotel. It was a happy, boisterous affair. Uncle Hector drank too much and insisted on singing, and Sally's mother's cousin had sniffed disapprovingly and said how typical of "those Morrisons" to lower the tone of things.

"She'd have liked champagne and canapés, and everyone circulating and making polite conversation," Sally said as they were leaving. "It was a good wedding. It was fun and everyone enjoyed it. That's what counts, isn't it?"

THEY'D gone off to Arran for their honeymoon and had an idyllic week, with days spent walking the hills and beaches of that enchanted isle, and evenings in the cosy little log-fires-and-copper bar of the hotel, talking and laughing and planning their future.

Happy ever after, that's how it was going to be. For them the wonder would never fade, the gloss would never wear off. They would be the prince and princess for all time, their love remaining as new and fresh as an early-morning rose.

So what had happened? Now, nine years later, why wasn't it like that?

Was it inevitable that marriage came to this, he wondered. To reheated dinners and food mixers to be fixed? To niggling and sniping at each other?

To being more interested in listening to a television programme than hearing about your partner's day?

Maybe it was. Maybe Tom had expected too much, gone into marriage like a teenage girl, head filled with all the golden promises of romance magazines.

Maybe in the end it always came down to routine, and coping, and getting along together as best you could.

It was difficult to be romantic when a baby was teething, and a five-year-old clamouring for a story.

Fairy-tales seemed a long way off when you were worrying about the mortgage, and the unopened bills that sat malevolently on the mantelpiece.

THE last year hadn't been easy. It was nine months now since he'd been made redundant from Jeffersons, and although he'd been lucky enough to get another job almost immediately, it wasn't the same. For one thing, the salary was less, adding a strain to the budget that had already been tight with Alistair's unplanned arrival.

And the work was different, too — with less regular hours and more pressure to succeed.

On top of that, there were his new colleagues. He had been one of the younger salesmen at Jeffersons. Now the position was reversed and Tom found himself out with guys like Chris Campbell and Jim Mulholland.

Young men. Single men, with money in their pockets and time to spare.

Men who could go for a pint after work without feeling guilty.

Men who could talk about Jane, or Penny, or Loretta — or whichever bright young thing had caught their attention at the weekend's club.

ONCE, they had asked him to go along with them. But though he'd been tempted for a moment, it wouldn't have done. He had seen one or two guys at Jeffersons go down that road. It wasn't for him. What would he have to say to girls of 19 with short skirts and highlighted hair — except to tell them how Heather was settling in at school, or how many teeth Alistair had cut now?

"Daddy, you're mumbling. I can't hear you prop'ly."

Heather's voice was sleepy-sounding. She had snuggled down in her bed, and Tom smoothed out her pillow.

Of course, it couldn't exactly have been easy for Sally either, he supposed.

She was the one who had to manage from day to day, saving a penny here, a penny there, wondering if there would be too much month left at the end of the housekeeping money.

There was never really anything left over for fancy clothes or make-up, or the occasional bottle of perfume.

Sally was the same age as Veronica Murray, the secretary in the office.

Ronni always looked like she'd stepped out of a fashion magazine, with beautifully-cut clothes and carefully-matched accessories.

Her hair was groomed to perfection, and she invariably smelled of the same expensive scent.

Tom had passed her desk yesterday and found himself wondering why Sally couldn't look like that. Sally was prettier than Ronni, who underneath the make-up really wasn't anything special.

A wave of guilt descended on him now. It was *his* fault Sally didn't look like that. Ronni had a good salary, and no home to look after, or husband or kids to tend.

Sally spent her days running around after his three children, and making sure that he had a fresh shirt for the morning, and that the house was always clean, if not always tidy.

Sally was nursemaid, laundry-woman, cleaner, housekeeper and cook.

She did all that, and he had the nerve to expect her groomed and perfumed and smiling when he returned home, all ready to sit and smooth his fevered brow and tell him how wonderful he was!

He wondered if she sometimes felt like turning the clock back, going back to those once-upon-a-time days with no worries and responsibilities. She never said so, but then there were so many things that he didn't talk about either.

Maybe that was the trouble with both of them.

Once they had talked so much, shared every little thing, so that nothing got out of proportion, nothing built up and chiselled away at them inside.

Now there never seemed to be time to talk. Or perhaps now they just never *made* time for each other.

"And so the prince and princess lived happily ever after," Tom finished.

He looked down at his daughter, but the happy ending had come too late for Heather.

She was fast asleep with her thumb in her mouth, and Miko the monkey held tightly in the crook of her arm.

Tom tucked the bedclothes around her and dropped a kiss on her forehead, then he glanced into the other room.

Iain was muttering happily in his sleep, and Alistair, sore gums forgotten, lay flat on his back, dead to the world.

HE went down to the kitchen. Sally had left his chop and potatoes on a low heat, and he ate them quickly. She was dozing when he went through to the living-room. Tom knelt in front of the chair and watched her silently.

A lock of hair had fallen across her face — obviously irritating her, for she kept turning her head to brush it away.

She was beautiful. He hadn't looked at her properly for such a long time. He had forgotten how beautiful she really was.

Tom felt a rush of emotion so strong it almost choked him.

He loved her. He loved her so much, although the day-by-day, minute-to-minute *awareness* of that love had gone.

Sally's head slipped back on the chair, and her expression was exactly the same as those on the faces of the children asleep upstairs.

Sally moved again, and her eyes opened.

"Hello, you." Tom smiled.

She looked back vaguely at him, with the puzzled eyes of one who has just woken.

"Sal, let's ask your mother if she'll come over and stay with the kids on Saturday, and we'll go to the Manor House over at Grangeleigh.

"Please?"

He stroked her cheek with his hand, and she caught it and pressed his fingers to her mouth.

"OK, then. We'll do that. Will I phone Mum now?"

"Tomorrow," Tom said. "Just now I want to tell you a story.

"It's about a beautiful princess, and a nasty, bad-tempered old prince who loved her very much, although he was sometimes too stupid and preoccupied to show it . . ."

Sally wound her arms round his neck.

"Let's make it a bedtime story," she said. "You can tell me upstairs." ■

A Fine

Arrangement

by Suzanne Thorpe

She worked in an office, he stayed at home. To begin with, it worked well. Then the trouble started...

I'VE just waxed the floor!" Emma stopped to gaze at her husband, Tom. It was a tense moment. Toby and Laurie were squabbling over TV channels in the next room. It was the school holidays, a rainy August day, and those splodgy grey footprints over the lemon and white kitchen floor were the last straw.

"Sorry, love," Emma said, putting her briefcase on the Welsh dresser. "I didn't realise it was floor day."

Tom looked petulant, frowning disapprovingly at her abandoned briefcase. Then he busied himself at the eye-level oven, checking the casserole. The crocodile oven mitts looked ridiculous on his big hands.

"Thursday is always my floor day," he said sullenly.

Emma bit back a smile, and then realised it wasn't that funny.

"Tom — playing mother and housewife!" All their friends had thought it a joke.

"It's a mutual and practical decision," Emma had explained, over and over again, "now he's been made redundant and the vacancy has cropped up for me at my old estate agency."

"But we mean — Tom!" they had chorused in turn.

Yes, Tom; all six foot, rugger-loving, fun-loving inch of him.

And lately she had been re-explaining that reason over and over to herself — it's a mutual and practical decision . . .

Looking at him now, in his crocodile mitts, the casserole a mystery of life to him, she wanted to cry.

Oh Tom, she thought. *What have I done to you?*

"That looks fine, love. Why don't you leave it for now? You look as if you've had enough for today," she coaxed.

But Tom wasn't so easily convinced. He was a perfectionist but it had always been with car engines and paint jobs before.

"It doesn't look fine. It's a mess. I spent an hour on it, you know!"

Emma gave up. She shrugged a surrender and tried to melt him with a smile instead.

"Sor-ree!"

Tom didn't laugh. "This isn't a joke —"

"Tom!" Now she was pleading. She was scared and angry at the same time.

What had happened to her madcap husband who used to tease her about having the cleanest dustbin in the avenue — about her rinsing out tin cans before throwing them away?

Where had her loveable giant gone — the man who kept the children in fits of laughter with the corniest knock-knock jokes in town?

EMMA brushed past Tom to put the kettle on, aware it was a covert act of defiance in what was now his domain. "Look, Tom, I've been in a menagerie full of bears all day — and they've all had sore heads, too. I don't need this when I get home!"

Right now she desperately needed her Tom — her loving, it'll-all-be-all-right husband whom she had always accused of being too easy-going.

He had always been the type to let people jump him in queues, to return snappy service in shops and restaurants with a smile.

This man, this stranger in her home, was as stubborn and dark as an ink stain on a white shirt.

"Well, excuse *me*," he retorted, his voice tight with sarcasm.

"Don't you think I get cheesed off, cooped up here all day? Doing the same jobs over and over again!

"Painting the Forth Bridge has nothing on this house!"

Emma felt an explosion of hurtful retorts brewing up inside her, when a small voice put out the fuse lit between them.

"Mummy?" It was Toby, standing in the doorway.

Emma gently scooped her six-year-old son up into her arms, as much to comfort herself as him.

"Don't look so glum — Mummy and Daddy are only talking, sweetheart."

The little boy looked from one to the other of his parents.

Tom sighed resignedly, tousling his son's dark hair absent-mindedly.

But Toby was more curious than upset. And he refused to be so easily fobbed off.

"You're not talking! You're squabsing again!" That was the children's word for row and squabbles and it made Tom and Emma exchange guilty looks.

"Nonsense, darling — it's only a game!"

"You were — you were! But you're both saying the wrong things!"

That was a stunner. It made Tom sit down suddenly at the pine table. Emma put Toby down and patted his rump affectionately.

"Now scoot and see the end of the cartoon!"

He trotted off, the "squabsing" already forgotten in favour of the Pink Panther and all his other cartoon favourites.

Emma busied herself at the oven, doing needless things to the casserole, while Tom said nothing, sitting immobile behind her.

She couldn't bear to see her husband look so defeated like that. He had always been so strong, had such sturdy shoulders.

He had supported her through the kids' childhood ailments, through her own father's death, and through their early years of scrimping and saving.

She had never seen him so demoralised before and it really frightened her.

"Mmm — smells wonderful — you're getting to be a real cordon bleu chef!" She put the lid back on the casserole, biting her lip. She had sounded much too patronising, much too tense.

Tom didn't answer, or even look up from the redundant hands which he was busy steepling together over the pine table.

Emma could bear it no longer and went to loop her arms around his neck, planting a kiss on his left earlobe.

TOM flinched. His ear had always been vulnerable but now it only seemed to cause him irritation. "You prepared it all last night," he said grudgingly, coming back to the casserole. "I only put it in the oven." She let her arms fall away and, feeling her move from him, he looked up at last.

"It's not working, is it, Emma?" The anxious look she passed him back was his answer.

No, it wasn't working at all.

They put a brave face on everything throughout the meal. But then, with two lively children they couldn't help but forget their problems for a while.

After dinner, Emma suggested Tom bathe Toby and Laurie. That had always been a special treat after he had been away from them all day and it might lift his spirits.

Then he reminded her that he *had* been with them all day and that *she* was the one who needed to spend some time with them.

So, wearily, she took care of baths and bed and he washed the dishes.

The twins tucked away and kissed goodnight, Emma went downstairs to find Tom much mellowed. He was sitting on the sofa with a brandy glass in his hand and one awaiting her on the coffee table.

She smiled then, and wriggled her way under his sweatered arm, and into his thoughts, warming as she felt their love melt around her.

This was Tom — her Tom, back again.

They sipped their brandies and stared at dusk glowing pink on the patio, behind a silhouette of apple boughs. Emma wished they could just stay that way, for days, weeks, and forget everything . . .

But facts had to be faced.

"Toby could see it." Tom spoke at last, slowly and thoughtfully. Emma felt stupidly blank.

"See what?"

"When he said we were saying the wrong things." Emma nodded. Yes, she remembered that and it had puzzled her.

"Well," Tom explained. "He didn't mean we were arguing, he meant we were saying the wrong things. You were moaning my moans and I was moaning your usual beefs!"

Emma thought it over a minute and realised Tom — and Toby, were both nerve-tinglingly right.

"Gosh — aren't kids amazing! Toby could see it and we couldn't!"

They both took long moments, and several sips of brandy, to mull this over and wonder how on earth to handle it.

"It's funny though, isn't it . . .?" Emma mused. "Ironic really. I mean, you'd think that by swapping rôles — and problems, we'd be able to understand each other's point of view better. But we don't, do we?"

"Human nature, I suppose . . ." Tom sighed again.

"I *do* understand how you feel though, love. I know how frustrating all this is for you. I have been married to you for ten years — of course I know how you feel."

"But do you — do you *really* understand?" He was angry again and released her carelessly to pace the hearth rug like a caged animal.

"I'm a father and a husband. I should be providing for my family!"

"But you do! You've always worked — and hard too, and goodness knows you've been after enough jobs since your redundancy.

"And you are doing a job now, my job. Or isn't motherhood and home-running classed as one?" Now she was getting angry, too.

"Don't get on your soap-box, you know what I mean. Don't tell me you're not getting satisfaction at going out into the world and playing at bread-winner?"

It was a cruel shot and she felt hurt. So that's what he was thinking.

"Tom . . ." But she could say no more. He was still pacing, still angry, insensitive to the painful thoughts running through her head.

How could he think that?

At first, maybe for a month or so, going out to work had been a novelty for Emma.

She had bought a new suit, a navy pinstripe with pencil skirt which accentuated her slim, blond looks, and borrowed Tom's tan briefcase.

It was like being 20 again and out of college, but having confidence and experience to back her up.

Then the novelty began to wear thin. It was just a job after all, a daily grind. She began to miss home and wonder what was going on there — especially as the schools broke up for the holidays.

Suddenly, she realised she didn't want to be a secretary or a career girl. She was a wife and a mother. That was her job and she enjoyed it.

She began to feel she'd lost part of her womanhood when she lost these rôles. Just as her husband felt he had lost his manhood when he lost his rôle as provider.

"You know what I daydreamed about the other afternoon?" she asked.

"No . . ."

He didn't sound as if he particularly cared. "A cake," she said flatly. That made him stop his pacing and caught his attention. "One of my sponges, with butter cream filling, in my own kitchen, from my own recipe and not one of those quick packet jobs. Scones, too, warm from the oven.

"And collecting the twins from school . . . watching 'Blue Peter' with them . . ."

She couldn't go on. Her voice became thick with emotion and she shielded her eyes, and her tears, with a hand.

Tom would think she had cracked up — crying over a cake!

But he put down his drink and rushed back to the sofa, pulling her into his chest and cradling her, the way he had when her father had died, and when the twins were suffering with measles and she had been suffering, too.

Should he confess that he had been reading the local papers for hours during the mornings, he wondered, inventing imaginary sales drives for the companies in the business section and feeling guilty, like an overgrown child playing a game?

"What are we going to do, Tom?"

"I don't know , love . . ." he whispered into her hair. "I really don't know . . ." He sounded so despairing.

The next day held more trouble for Emma at the office.

"I've good news for you — and bad," Henry, her boss, declared.

She had first started work for him when she was a graduate from secretarial college and had been daunted by his gruff manner. Only later had she found a shy, middle-aged bachelor hiding behind it.

The result had been a happy and efficient working partnership which had ended when Emma gave up work during her pregnancy.

So she merely raised an eyebrow to question what the news was, knowing his droll sense of humour only too well.

"The good news is — I'm leaving! But the bad news, for you, is that I'll still be in the company." She forgot the instant coffee she was preparing and whirled round to face him.

"It's not good news that you're leaving!"

SHE felt disappointed and it showed. He shrugged and she caught a tinge of disappointment in his own eyes — she should have known he would hide his feelings behind a joke or two. "But you are staying in the company?" she asked. He nodded.

"Alex wants me to be co-director with him . . ." he said, almost shyly.

"But that's great!"

"You won't be saying that next week — when you're up to your eyes in the marketing for Grovewood Homes and I want you to start answering applications and arranging interviews!"

"When have I ever complained of hard work? Does that mean I'll have a new boss, then? Are we going to advertise? You'll want an advert, in the 'Evening News' of course." She began writing.

"Head it 'New Developments Manager' . . ." Henry paused, then shook his head.

"Of course, it's just a formality, isn't it? Advertising, I mean. I dare say the company already have someone in mind to take my place — some young whizz kid with too many ideas and not enough experience . . ."

Emma stared at Henry, her mind racing. What was it Tom had said?

"What's it worth these days — all this experience and hard work?" Of course! Tom!

"Tom's experienced in management," she blurted out. "He could do this job, I know he could. Do you think . . .?"

But Henry held up his hand, his face full of sympathy. "Hold it, Emma. I know how you must feel. Maybe I shouldn't tell you, but I happen to know there *is* someone earmarked for my place already. I'm sorry."

Emma nodded slowly. They were silent for a moment. Then Henry looked at her intently.

"Look, I don't know how you'd feel about this, but there is another position coming up — a junior post, the salary isn't too high. Maybe Tom would feel he's above it, but it would be a start. He could work his way up. If I used my newly-found influence, I'm sure I could get it for him . . ."

"WINE? My goodness, you are doing us proud tonight!" Emma said. She gazed at the table, decked with a vase of flowers and two red candles in the silver holders that had belonged to her mother. She took her briefcase into the hall. Tom flung aside the crocodile mitts to loop his arms around her waist when she returned to the kitchen.

"Tired?" She shook her head and returned the kiss he had just given her.

"No, I had a great day, actually. Henry was busy, so I showed some nice people around the first Grovewood Home and sold it!"

"Terrific! That's it — pave the way for the old man!"

They both laughed, basking in the wonderful, warm feeling that had revived between them lately — that good, old feeling they had missed so much.

Tom pulled Emma closer to him and they kissed, longer and with more feeling than they had ever done before at six o'clock in the evening.

They were interrupted by a squeal.

A glance told them two pairs of exploring hands were trying to identify the little pink things atop the avocados.

"Ah-ah!" Emma pulled the little hands away and hugged her children.

"The terrors have already eaten," Tom said. "And I trust everything was in order for Mademoiselle and Monsieur?"

He gave an ingratiating bow which produced a round-eyed stare from Toby and a chuckle from his sister. Emma smiled happily. This was her old Tom back again.

"Do you want to bath the kids while I see to the Chicken Kiev?"

"Chicken Kiev — how wonderful!"

"Supermarket frozen, actually."

"Still wonderful. You see to the kids, though, love. After all, I'll have to get back in harness in the kitchen, won't I?" He looked suddenly serious again and understood her meaning.

"Come on, terrors . . ." He hoisted a child up in each arm and took them upstairs.

He had remembered that when he started his new job as Sales Manager he would be arriving home late. Even to see his children awake, then, would be a bonus.

But for that week, since Henry had offered him the job and Emma had given in her notice, they had been in a delightful no-man's-land where both were able to remember the rôles they had left, their joys and problems.

Tom had been enjoying his last taste of housewifery — for a lifetime he hoped, while Emma had been savouring her last taste of a career, for a few years, at least.

But she wasn't kidding herself, as she took Tom's supermarket chicken out of the oven, that the mutual consideration phase would last.

When the rôles changed back no doubt the old moans would change back, too.

"YOU might have phoned to let me know you'd be late!" Tom gave her one of his tired, not-that-again looks. He left his briefcase on the dresser and poured himself a coffee from the percolator. Emma went to whisk the case into the hall but was stopped by Laurie appearing in the doorway in her nightgown. She was allowed to join her brother on Tom's knee.

"Daddy had to work late . . ." he was saying.

"Why?" Laurie asked pertly.

"Why?" Toby chorused.

Why? Emma thought angrily. Why couldn't he just ring and save the chops from cremation?

But she felt sorry when she saw the red rims of tiredness around his eyes. He was putting everything into learning the property business.

"I only hope the chops aren't spoiled . . ." Her tone had softened and was almost apologetic.

"Anything will be fine," Tom said. "Daddy *is* sorry!" He was talking to the twins but she knew the apology was meant for her, too.

"*Now* you're saying the right things," Toby said chirpily. "Now you are . . ."

It took a moment for it to sink in, before Emma turned, smiling, and threw down the crocodile mitts in surrender. Tom was seeing the funny side, too, and tired and disgruntled as he was, he managed a chuckle.

"What is it, Daddy?" Laurie asked, hanging her arms around his neck to peer closer into his face.

"Nothing, darling —" He laughed openly now, and Emma joined him, crossing the room to plant a kiss on his brow. The twins were shrieking with laughter, too, only they didn't know why.

"We *are* saying the right things!" Emma laughed.

For at least now they could see the funny side, even though they would go on the rest of their lives saying the right things and bemoaning the same complaints — the complaints of love. ■

The Chill Of Summer Love

by Isobel Stewart

**Once you've met the most important person
in your life — how do you let him go?**

I HEARD an old song today as I thought of you. Do you remember it — 'Unforgettable'? As soon as I heard it, I wondered how it could have happened that I'd forgotten you. No, not forgotten you exactly, just — not thought of you, not missed you, not wondered about you, for so long.

As I stood in my bright, sun-filled kitchen, listening to the song that would always remind me of you, I thought of that golden summer when you'd been my whole life.

I was 17 and had just finished school. At the end of the holidays I was to start nursing and was both excited and apprehensive at the new life ahead.

Childhood was behind me and womanhood lay ahead.

My aunt had invited me to join her and her family at their beach house, as I'd often done before.

But I told my mother I'd rather stay at home on the farm — I wanted to be by myself.

I wanted to walk around the farm, I wanted to touch the animals — I wanted to gather a little store of memories to draw on.

At least, that was what I wanted until you came along. Then all I wanted was to be with you.

You were so different from anyone I had known.

Older, probably 10 years older than me, and certainly older than any of the boys who took me to the youth club dances.

I couldn't quite decide, that first time, when I watched you working with the cow my father was worried about, your hair touched by the sunlight, whether you were like a young Robert Redford or a young Paul Newman.

"Yes, it is a tumour," you said to my father. "It should be fairly straightforward, though."

65

I watched your hands, strong and sure, as you gave the cow an injection.

Just then I realised that I'd almost missed being there.

Even when my father had told me that Tom Anderson's locum was coming, I hadn't really listened.

"Jenny, you could bring us a cup of tea while we're waiting," my father said.

"Or would you rather have coffee, Mr Russell?"

You smiled at me and I realised how blue your eyes were, in the brown of your face.

"Tea, thanks," you said. "And it's Steve."

Afterwards I watched you and listened to you.

And I knew, right then, that I loved you.

There was a feeling of rightness, of certainty.

You had to come back a couple of times after that, and each time I waited, almost afraid to be with you again in case I'd just imagined the way you were and the way I felt about you.

But I hadn't imagined anything — you were the man I loved.

On your second visit, you mentioned casually that you were having trouble finding someone to help with your afternoon surgery.

I thought about it and, the next time you came I said, just as casually as you had, that I wouldn't mind helping if you were stuck.

"I thought you were planning a lazy summer, Jen," my father said. "Your last long holiday, remember."

"I'll still have the mornings to do what I want," I replied quickly.

"I'd enjoy helping, Steve. It would still be nursing experience even if the patients are four-legged instead of two-legged!"

You smiled the slow, warm smile that made you look younger and took that strange shadow from your eyes.

"You might find you prefer the four-legged patients, Jenny," you joked.

"Look, if you're prepared to give up your afternoons, I'd be very grateful."

THE golden days of that summer went on. Perhaps there were grey, cloudy days but I don't remember any. I used to get up early and go for long walks, seldom meeting anyone and preferring not to. I was content just to walk and dream, to think of you and to wait for the two hours in the afternoon when we would be together.

You were such a good vet. I realised that very quickly.

Your hands were strong and gentle, yet you spoke softly and kindly to a nervous cat or dog.

The first day, as soon as surgery was over, I made tea.

"You don't have to, Jenny," you said, smiling down at me.

"Your work's done and you've left everything clean and tidy.

"I'm off on some calls now."

"Then I'm sure you can do with a cup of tea before you go," I replied, conscious of the warm colour in my cheeks.

After that, I made tea every day, knowing you barely had time to drink it but wanting to keep you with me just a few moments longer.

One afternoon, I arrived home to find my mother looking out for me. Her manner didn't seem natural.

"You're later than I thought you would be, Jenny," she said.

There was something in her tone of voice that made me look closely at her, as I leaned my bike against the wall.

"Hot day for cycling," I replied, ignoring her comment.

I went into the kitchen and poured a glass of water.

When I set the glass down, I noticed my mother was looking at me in a strange way.

"I was talking to Tom Anderson's sister today," she said a little abruptly.

"She happened to mention Steve Russell. I was surprised to hear that he's married."

Carefully, I set my glass down at the sink. I didn't say anything because I wasn't sure if I could.

My hands, I saw with a strange detachment, were trembling.

"Aren't you surprised, Jenny?" my mother asked.

"Or perhaps he's mentioned his wife?"

"No," I said, grateful to find my voice quite steady. "No, he hasn't mentioned his wife."

And then, because she was still looking at me and I couldn't bear the concern and pity in her eyes, I said quite sharply, "But neither has he done or said anything out of keeping with his being married."

And that was the truth. I'd longed for our hands to brush together and our eyes to meet, but I hadn't been impatient.

There was a long, golden summer ahead of us when I'd felt sure you would come to realise what I'd known so quickly.

"I wonder where his wife is?" I said, my voice clear and light.

"I must remember to ask him some time."

NEXT day, when we were having our cup of tea after surgery, I dropped the subject casually into our conversation. "Pity your wife isn't here with you, Steve. Is she working and can't get away?" I saw the momentary tightening of your hand on the cup and the wary look in your eyes.

"No," you said carefully. "No, she's spending a couple of weeks with her parents — they have a farm in Wales.

"Once a farm girl always a farm girl, Jenny, you'll find that.

"I thought it would do Katherine good to spend the summer with her folk."

And then, with what seemed like a sudden decision, you put your cup down. "No," you said loudly. "That isn't really the way it is.

"We're friends but I haven't spoken about Katherine to you because it was easier not to.

"Six months ago," you began bleakly, "we lost the baby we were expecting.

"He lived just a few moments. Perhaps that was worse really because Katherine thought everything was all right."

I wanted to touch your hand but you were too far away from me and your grief had nothing to do with me.

"We were both sad and upset but you have to get on with living.

"Somehow, Katherine just hasn't been able to. She's just a shell of herself, has no interest in anything, no life, no hope.

"We could have another baby — the doctor says that, physically, she's well enough now. But she just says 'not yet'.

"I thought it would do us both good to get right away and this temporary job seemed ideal.

"But she got very upset at the thought of coming to a strange place and meeting new people."

You looked at me, and I could have wept for the hurt and bewilderment on your dear face. "I asked her what she wanted to do and she simply said, 'Go home.' So she went."

I kept thinking about what you'd told me.

I couldn't understand how she could turn from you, how she could hold on to her grief and not see that you needed her, too.

Later, I casually told my mother that your wife was spending some time with her family, that you'd talked to me about her and that her name was Katherine.

My mother was wise and loving. She neither questioned me further, nor suggested that I stop working for you.

All she did was remind me that my aunt's offer of joining her at the seaside still stood.

But, of course, I didn't want to go. The long, golden summer was almost halfway through and I wanted to spend every moment of it near you.

Sometimes, you spoke of Katherine, and I listened.

But, at other times, you spoke just to me, and there was no shadow of Katherine between us.

THE day of the church fête dawned bright and sunny. I don't think there had been a day quite as perfect as that one. We were together almost every moment. You were judging the pets' parade and asked me to help you.

At the end of it all, when the prizes had been awarded, you took me to have tea and scones.

I deserved it, you said, because I'd been such a help to you, not only that day but all through the time we had worked together.

When you said that, I felt my throat tighten; it was as if you were rewarding a child for being good.

Oh, I'd always realised that you didn't know I loved you — I didn't want you to know — but, suddenly, I realised just how you did see me.

I was Jim Dale's daughter Jenny, a nice, sympathetic girl — but not a woman like your Katherine.

I poured a second cup of tea and, as I passed it to you, my misery was replaced by concern for you.

"You're far away, Steve," I said with difficulty.

You smiled mechanically, without warmth in your eyes.

"I'm sorry, Jenny." Your voice was soft. "I was thinking about Katherine, wondering if she's missing me as much as I'm missing her.

"Is she feeling any different, or is she just relieved to be on her own, away from me?"

"Have you asked her?" I wanted to know. "In a letter, or on the phone?"

"No," you said, after a moment, obviously surprised.

"No, I write very careful letters, telling her what I'm doing.

"I just say that I hope she's feeling better. She needs time."

I leaned forward. "She needs to be told just how you feel," I said firmly.

"She needs to know that you miss her, that you love her and — maybe even that it's time she stopped grieving and started living again."

You shook your head. "I don't know," you said after a while.

"I don't think it would do any good, Jenny."

I pointed out that it wasn't doing much good just sitting waiting to see how Katherine felt.

And then — not very easily and without looking at you — I told you that if I was Katherine, knowing how *you* were feeling might make the world of difference.

"Oh, she knows how I feel," you replied a little bitterly.

"She just doesn't seem to care, about me or about anything."

"Then make her care," I told you. "Go to her, give her a good shake, make her look at you and listen to you, Steve."

You smiled then.

"You are a determined little thing, Jenny," you said. "Well, I'll think about it.

"And, thank you for caring."

We parted then but you said you would see me at the dance that night in the school hall.

You were late coming and I began to think that, perhaps, you had decided not to, or perhaps you'd had an emergency call.

I danced every dance because this was my home and I knew everyone. But, all the time, I was looking for you, wondering where you were.

And, then, when you did come I didn't see you until you were right beside me and the band was playing 'Unforgettable.'

Dancing with you, being close to you, was all I had dreamed it would be and more.

I wanted the dance and the magic of that old song to go on for the rest of my life.

"Jenny," you told me quietly. "I'm going to do what you said.

"I've got Harry Paton to take over at the practice for a couple of days, and I'm leaving tomorrow morning.

"I'm going to drive straight there and make Katherine listen to me."

"I'm so pleased, Steve," I said very clearly and very steadily. And then, to my horror, I began to cry.

"Jenny?" You looked so taken aback.

BUT, I just couldn't stop the tears. And, through them, I saw understanding slowly dawn in your face. Very firmly, you led me off the dance floor and out of the side door into the warm summer evening.

I don't think I even tried to stop the tears. For, right then, nothing would have stopped them.

You put your arms around me and held me close, not saying anything — just holding me.

And, when my tears were over you dried my face gently with your handkerchief.

"I'm sorry," I said, not quite steadily.

"No, Jenny," you said softly. "I'm sorry. I've been so self-centred.

"I never realised how you were feeling."

You didn't pretend not to know why I had wept and I was grateful for that, then and afterwards.

"I'll always remember this summer, Jenny. It hasn't been easy and most of the time it hasn't been very happy.

"But, the good moments I've had and the memories I'll treasure, are all thanks to you.

"Remember that, Jenny."

"What will *you* remember?" I asked you.

You looked down at me, and you smiled. And, in that one moment, there was no-one else, only you and me.

"I'll remember a girl called Jenny." Your voice was warm.

"A girl with hazel eyes and brown hair and freckles.

"A pretty girl who is so many things — funny, kind, caring and wise."

You kissed me then, your lips warm on mine for a moment.

And, from the open door, I could hear the words of the song, "*That someone so unforgettable thinks that I am unforgettable, too.*"

"Powder your nose, Jenny," you told me, "and go back in there. Dance with young Joe Powrie or the Johnson boy.

"Have fun, and keep your chin up."

I did it — because you asked me to. I even let Joe Powrie take me home but, when he put his arms around me, I turned aside so that his lips just brushed my cheek — for your kiss was still warm on my lips. I cried again when I was in bed but there was something healing in my tears this time because of the way you'd spoken to me.

I only saw you once more after that when you came to tell me that Katherine was coming home, that everything was going to be all right.

"I'm so glad," I said steadily, and I really meant it. For the shadow I had sometimes glimpsed had gone from your eyes.

I walked you to your car.

I was going to spend the last weeks of the summer with my cousins at the seaside, I'd decided. And then I said goodbye — very quickly — and went back into the house.

★　★　★　★

I suppose the rest of the summer was as golden as the first part had been. I know that, soon, I was as tanned as my cousins.

You had gone by the time I got home, you and Katherine.

I didn't ask about you and my mother didn't say anything.

But, a year later, when I'd passed my exams and come home for a short holiday, she told me that you and Katherine had just had a little girl.

Two years after that, I heard that you had a son.

Since then, I haven't heard anything more about you.

At first, I thought of you often — and then not so much.

But, from time to time, there was a stab of memory and I would feel once again the weight of losing you.

But, how can you lose something you've never really had?

Then, in my final year of nursing, I met Robert who was doing his internship. We were friends before we fell in love with each other and we're still both friends and lovers.

We have two sons and a daughter and my life is very full as a doctor's wife and as a mother of three young children.

I suppose that's why I was startled to hear that song and to realise that it was so long since I'd thought of you.

Yet, as the last strains of the song fade, I realise now that you are an intrinsic part of me.

You helped to make me the woman I am today.

No, I haven't really forgotten you.

But you are part of yesterday.

Today is what matters and, for me, today and all my tomorrows are here with my husband and our children.

But I'll always be glad of you and yesterday — and that long-ago, golden summer. ■

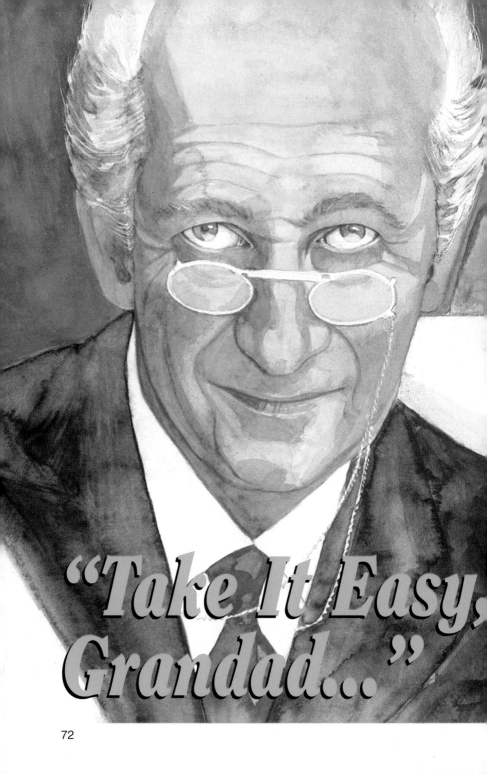

"Take It Easy, Grandad..."

It was ridiculous! The only time he was allowed to lift a finger was to tap out his boredom!

by Eileen Elias.

BOYS, I thought, were hopeless — especially younger brothers. The very first thing Geoff had said when Mother told us Grandpa Joe was coming to live with us was, "Great! No more yukky school dinners! Now we can come home at lunch-time."

"Oh no, you can't!" Mother had said briskly.

"If you think your grandpa's going to wait on you," she told him sternly, "you've another think coming.

"The doctor says he can't be expected to cope by himself any more, so what he needs is a bit of care and attention."

She paused, peeling the potatoes for our meal, and I saw her eyes take on that faraway look I had come to know.

"He's your dad's father after all, and your dad, if he had lived, would have been the first to invite him to come to us."

Young Geoff's face was puzzled. "I only meant — oh," he said petulantly, "why can't everything be the way it used to be?"

I saw Mother's face soften, and she reached across and ruffled his hair.

"Lots of things have to be different, now Dad's not with us," she said

73

gently. "Me going out to work, for one thing.

"But at least we've all got each other and now we're going to have Grandpa as well." She turned to me, a worried frown crossing her face.

"You'll have to help look after him, Una. He's had a hard life and it's time he took things easy."

Mother was obviously very anxious about poor Grandpa. Since Dad died she seemed to carry the whole world on her shoulders even when it wasn't really necessary.

Grandpa might be frail, but he'd never seemed old to me.

We called him Grandpa Joe to distinguish him from our other grandpa, Grandpa William, who lived a long way away. Grandpa William seemed really old; sort of buttoned-up and disapproving. But Grandpa Joe wasn't like that at all.

He had bright blue eyes which twinkled when he laughed. No, Grandpa Joe never seemed old at all.

But he must have seemed so to Mother. The very first day he came, she grabbed his suitcases from him and started up the stairs.

"Give those to me, Joe," she said briskly and confidently, no doubt trying to cover up the worried concern in her eyes. "Remember it's time for you to take things easy." She looked anxiously and meaningfully at us.

Ineffectually Grandpa tried to grab at the cases, but Mother was already away with them to the landing.

"Goodness gracious me, Mary!" That was one of his favourite sayings. "What do you think I am, letting a lady carry my cases?"

Mother took no notice, but showed Grandpa Joe his room. "I hope you'll be comfortable here, Joe. Just ask for anything you want.

"Una here will be bringing your breakfast tray up each morning before school, and Geoff will run out for your paper.

"And don't worry about Winston. He's happy in the yard, now he's got that nice warm kennel.

"No need to get up till long after I've gone to work, and I'll leave you a nice little lunch in the kitchen. Then you can take a turn in the garden, or have a nap till the children come home at four-fifteen."

Grandpa spluttered. "No need for all that, Mary. I can get up early, same as you. And I never have napped in the afternoons —"

Mother put a hand on his arm and looked into his twinkling blue eyes.

"Well," she said softly, "you've never really had the chance."

"Isn't there anything I could do to help?" he asked, rather plaintively, I thought.

"Yes, there is," Geoff put in. "You could —"

Mother nudged him and Geoff fell obediently silent.

Grandpa's eyes twinkled, and he rubbed his chin in the way he did when he had something to say and didn't quite know how to say it.

We left Grandpa Joe standing in the doorway, but I saw he made no move towards the bed. Instead he walked to the window and stood looking out, rubbing his chin again.

74

I went downstairs slowly, wondering what he was thinking. You never could tell with Grandpa Joe.

I wondered the same thing next morning when I brought him his breakfast tray. There he was, up and dressed, and staring out of the window again. I put his tray on the bedside table.

"I thought you'd still be asleep," I said.

"Not on your life!" Grandpa said. "I've risen at half-six for as long as I can remember. It's you young ones who like to lie abed."

I thought of Geoff, still hunched beneath the bedclothes. All the same I just didn't have the heart to tell Mother that Grandpa Joe didn't want his breakfast in bed.

H E sits about a lot, doesn't he?" Geoff observed that first week. "Old people do sit about," I told him. "At least, that's what Mother says." "Yes, but he doesn't like sitting. Look at the way he keeps drumming his fingers on the arm of his chair."

It was true. Grandpa Joe did sit about a lot, but it was a restless sort of sitting. He walked about outside sometimes, but it was a restless sort of walk, too.

Mother would fret about him wandering about so much in the garden, worried that he'd catch a cold.

But in the end it was Geoff who caught one — complete with sniffles, and the usual nasty cough and sore throat.

Dr Gordon came to examine him. And when he'd finished and reassured Mother it was nothing serious, he turned to Grandpa.

"Well, and how's the world treating you?" he asked.

"Fine," Grandpa Joe said.

"Not letting these kids wear you out?"

"These kids," Grandpa said, rubbing his chin, "wait on me hand and foot. Sometimes I wish they didn't."

Mother gave him a quizzical look and frowned, but didn't say anything.

"Ah," Dr Gordon said. "Well, you can't grumble at that." He paused.

"I don't know if you're interested, Mr Jameson, but some of my elderly patients go to classes at the Centre down the road. Keep-fit for the over-sixties.

"It's on Wednesdays, I think." He winked at Grandpa Joe. "Get you out a bit, wouldn't it? And it's only a five-minute walk."

I saw Grandpa Joe give him a thoughtful look. "I wouldn't mind giving it a try," he said with enthusiasm.

"Oh but, Joe," Mother put in hastily, "are you sure that would be a good idea? You know how —"

"Do him the world of good, Mrs Jameson," Dr Gordon interjected.

"Well," Mother said, "we'll see."

And we did. The very next week Grandpa Joe went to enrol.

We arrived home from school as soon as we could the following Wednesday, all agog to see how Grandpa Joe had fared.

He was in the little kitchen brewing himself a cup of tea, and he certainly looked sprightly, and not at all tired.

Maybe Dr Gordon was right, I thought. He did seem a bit cheerier.

He was. Even Mother had to agree.

There was a new sparkle in his blue eyes, and his shoulders were no longer bent.

"Tell us what it's like, Grandpa Joe," begged Geoff. "Did you do a lot of 'bend and stretch'?"

Grandpa Joe chuckled. "A man likes to have some secrets, laddie. Ask no questions and you'll be told no lies," he added, tapping the side of his nose.

"I only wanted to know —" Geoff persisted, till Mother gave him a look.

"Leave your grandpa alone, there's a dear," she said. "He'll tell us in his own good time." She glanced across at Grandpa Joe. "I — I do hope it isn't going to tire you, Joe."

"Goodness gracious me, Mary," Joe said. "I'm not done for yet, you know!"

And that seemed enough to keep Mother quiet.

After that, Grandpa Joe walked about the house like a dog with two tails. And when Mother came home from work, he followed her round like a dog. He was worse than Winston!

One day I watched him, as he watched Mother lining a plate with pastry and filling it with meat.

He smiled as she wetted the edges and pressed down the crust, then opened the oven door and popped in the pie for our supper.

"Smells good, doesn't it?" he said as he sat at the kitchen table.

"It's good to see you taking an interest in your food again, Joe," Mother smiled.

"I only wish you didn't have to work so hard, Mary," Grandpa Joe said.

He flexed his muscles and grinned. "See — I'm fine, really — I'm sure I could help, no bother."

"Oh no, Joe!" Mother said, looking up quite flushed. "You really mustn't — you can't, and well —" she floundered. "I'll be getting a treat myself in a couple of weeks' time, anyway.

"It's my birthday and we're going out to supper. The one night in the whole year when I don't have to cook."

"Birthday, did you say?" He looked at her keenly.

"Mmm." Mother set the table with busy fingers.

"When John was alive, we always had a wonderful birthday meal. He cooked it himself, and we had candles and singing, and flowers — everything.

"But now — well, we just go down to Russell's Restaurant in the town." She sighed. "It's not like it used to be, but at least it makes a change."

Her voice tailed away, and Grandpa looked at her keenly. "Am I included in this birthday business?"

Mother smiled. "Of course you are, Joe. Your keep-fit class won't have started up again after the Christmas break, so you shouldn't be too tired."

"When are you going to give us a demonstration, Grandpa?" Geoff asked cheekily.

Grandpa rubbed his chin, and Mother's cheeks went pink.

"You do your keep-fit to music, don't you? I could play you something on my mouth-organ," Geoff offered, unabashed.

Grandpa pretended to shudder.

"Don't worry your grandfather," Mother said. "He doesn't want to be bullied by you children." But we saw his blue eyes were twinkling.

"Maybe I'll give you that demonstration," he said. "When the time comes, but not before.

"Yes, yes, I'll give you a demonstration all right," he added confidently. "On your ma's birthday — and that's a promise."

His eyes twinkled with life and I couldn't help thinking that Dr Gordon couldn't have given him any better medicine.

Christmas came and went and though sometimes Grandpa looked a bit restless, nobody said anything. We all knew he'd be all right once his classes started again.

No, it was Ma who looked tired these days. Christmas has been good fun, but a lot of work for her.

THE morning of Mother's birthday, I took Grandpa's breakfast tray up, as usual. But, as always, he was already dressed and standing by the window gazing out. He looked quite young, I thought, and excited, too. Perhaps he was thinking ahead to Mother's birthday treat tonight.

"Got your birthday presents for your ma, have you?" he said as I put down the tray.

"Yes, oh yes!" I told him. "I've got her some pretty hankies, and Geoff's bought some scent."

"I've got her something, too," Grandpa said. "But it'll have to wait till she gets home tonight." Suddenly his voice dropped.

"Listen, how d'you like to give her a big surprise?

"Go and meet her after school, with Geoff, and escort her home. Birthday style."

"You mean —?" I said. "Instead of coming home at four — we go and —?"

Grandpa nodded. "She says she's leaving early tonight. About half past four. You could bring her back and make her really feel grand.

"Then when she's rested, she'll be ready for the evening.

"Eh? What do you think? Her office isn't far from the school and you don't cross any roads."

I considered. We'd never done it before. But why not, I thought.

"Keep it a secret!" Grandpa urged. "It's to be a surprise, see?"

I ran downstairs to whisper to Geoff while Mother was busy in the kitchen.

But all the same, he nearly forgot when we came out of school together.

He was just running off home when I managed to catch him by the sleeve. "Geoff, you've forgotten. We're going to meet Mother from the office."

It seemed strange walking in the opposite direction from home, strange passing all the shops and offices, but it was exciting.

Before too long we saw Mother coming down the steps, and ran towards her.

Mother looked at us both with astonished eyes.

"Why," she cried as we took both her hands. "What's all this about?"

"We've come to meet you," Geoff said. "It's a surprise. A birthday surprise."

"And a very nice one," Mother said.

It was fun all three of us walking back along the road, past the school, fun walking up our road in the evening light, and turning in at our little front gate.

"What's Grandpa Joe given you?" Geoff asked as we went up the path.

Mother smiled. "He said to wait until tonight. I expect he's got a little something to give me before we got out to Russell's."

"And he promised something else," Geoff urged.

"Have you forgotten, Mother — Grandpa's going to show us his exercises. Bend and stretch, bend and stretch, while I play my mouth-organ. Remember?"

From the look on Mother's face it was hardly something she could forget.

He stopped abruptly, as Mother put her key in the door, and lifted his head.

We both did the same. There was a savoury smell as we entered the little hall. A distinct smell. A wonderful smell.

It was a bit like Russell's Restaurant, only nicer. Mother smiled indulgently.

"Grandpa's making himself something in the kitchen," she said.

She stepped forward towards the kitchen door, and then stopped and gasped, and so did we.

Grandpa Joe was standing in the middle of the floor, a striped apron round his ample waist, a ladle in his hand. And from the stove came that wonderful waft of — supper?

Geoff's eyes were round and Mother's cheeks were pinker than ever.

"What's this? You're cooking supper!" she cried.

"No rule against that, is there, Mary?"

Mother paused, unable to say any more, and Grandpa Joe turned her round and pointed her in the direction of the dining-room.

"You just go in there," he said, and his face was one big smile.

We all went through and stopped in amazement. The table was beautifully laid for dinner — dinner for four.

The white cloth was one of Mother's best, and the silver was best, too. Goodness knows where Grandpa had found it.

There were flowers — real flowers, not plastic ones like those at Russell's. And yes — there were candles. Tall and red, in tiny glass holders. The ones we had left over from Christmas.

Next to them, in place of honour, was a bottle of wine and four sparkling glasses.

Mother crumpled into a chair, and Geoff and I stood speechless.

Grandpa put his head round the door. "No need to go out now, Mary. You've everything you need here.

"Dinner'll be ready in twenty minutes — it's my present to you.

"It's called — let me see — goodness gracious me, I can't remember the name now. Something outlandish. Mouss — mouss —"

"Moussaka?" Mother put in, in a tremulous voice.

Grandpa nodded. "That's it. That's what she told me."

Mother looked up. "*Who* told you?"

"She did. The teacher, of course. Moussaka — that's what she said."

"But —" Mother spluttered. "What teacher?"

"The teacher at my class, of course," replied Grandpa matter-of-factly.

"But," Mother began again. "They don't teach cookery at keep-fit classes!"

Grandpa Joe rubbed his chin. "Who said anything about keep-fit classes?

"Nobody asked me whether I'd enrolled for keep-fit or whether it was something else. Keep-fit was Dr Gordon's idea, not mine.

"I wanted something different. Yes, and something useful. So I decided on the 'Cookery For Men' course — much more useful."

Mother took a deep breath. "Joe, you'll never fail to surprise me. Why didn't you tell us?"

Grandpa chuckled.

"I knew what you'd say, Mary. Take it easy, don't help around the house, don't bother."

Mother opened her mouth to protest but Grandpa wouldn't let her.

"Well, now I've proved I'm perfectly capable of giving you a helping hand," he beamed.

Mother's eyes were full as she gazed up at him.

"Oh, Joe! Joe, it's — it's like old times!"

AND it *was* like old times. Geoff was too young to remember, but I did. We sat down, and ate Grandpa Joe's moussaka, we clinked glasses, and lit candles, watched Mother blow them out, and sang "Happy Birthday" just as we'd done years ago.

"Better than a demonstration of keep-fit, eh, Geoff?" Grandpa said when the last candle was blown out.

"Cept that I wanted to play my mouth-organ," Geoff said huffily.

Grandpa chuckled, "Play away! It's an occasion like this that calls for some music."

So Geoff played and played until we'd all lapsed into a tired and happy silence. Geoff sank against Mother's shoulder as she sat at the table, and I saw a faraway look in his eyes.

Mother cuddled him close.

"I was just wondering," Geoff said dreamily. "Was this the way it used to be — on your birthday I mean?"

Mother's eyes met mine and Grandpa's.

"Yes, Geoff," she said very low. "Well, nearly. As nearly as it can be."

"Good," Geoff murmured sleepily. "Know what, Mother? Now Grandpa Joe can cook, we can come home at lunch-time. No more yukky school dinners!"

"Geoff!" Mother scolded.

"Goodness gracious me!" Grandpa Joe said. "That's an idea now. Shouldn't wonder if the little chap's right, Mary — eh?"

And he was. ∎

The Hallowe

How could she make it clear that he was the one guest who should never have been invited?

en Party by Dorothy L. Garrard

T'S Dad," Evelyn explained over the phone. "Nothing to worry about, but the doctor finally whisked him into hospital to have his arthritis seen to." "Oh — poor old Dad," Audrey began. "He won't like that." "'Poor old Dad'? Don't waste your sympathy! He didn't say a word about going in when I phoned him last week — and I think he'd have kept us in the dark altogether if he'd had the chance."

Audrey smiled. Dad fancied himself as the spriteliest OAP in the country. "He needs rest and care," Evelyn explained.

"When the hospital said he could go home if there was someone to look after him, he jumped at the chance.

"Only I'm sure he had no intention of calling me. He expected to be able to get up and skip around like a two-year-old once they took their eyes off him.

"He sounded so aggrieved at being weak and wobbly that it was quite comical, really. Anyhow, I'm going up to Merton on Friday."

"Is Liz going with you?"

"No, and that's the other reason I rang. She's well into her 'A'-level course and you know she isn't exactly the world's most dedicated student. Also, she's arranging a Hallowe'en party while I'm away.

"I'd just prefer it if there was someone responsible around to keep an eye on her.

"Besides . . ." Evelyn hesitated. "I can't really go into details over the phone, but she's met this young man. It's just an infatuation, of course, but she talks about nothing else."

"Evelyn, I —"

"Oh, I know she's turned seventeen and it all has to happen eventually. But this one's too old for her in more ways than one.

"She's always listened to you, Audrey," she said persuasively. "She thinks of you more as a sister than an aunt, being so much nearer in age.

"She's being rebellious about school, too," Evelyn went on, a plea in her tone now. "I'm sure it's connected with him, somehow.

"Audrey, please, I'm pinning my hopes on you making her see sense . . ."

"Well, if you put it like that — of course," Audrey agreed.

"Oh, I *am* glad — and not only because of Dad and Liz. You haven't been up to see us for ages. We've all missed you.

"I bet Mark's at the bottom of it. You can't go on hiding him away, you know. Why not bring him with you, and stay on after I get back?"

"I'm afraid you won't meet Mark now," she said quietly. "We split up.

"I — I ought to have told you earlier, but I didn't like to talk about it."

She had never been able to put it into words — her feelings for Mark. Especially with Evelyn, whose late husband, Ted, had been as loyal and straightforward as she was.

Audrey had met Mark Simmonds the previous November, when she accompanied her boss to a conference. Tall, dark and exciting, he had lifted her out of her quietly pleasant existence and showed her another, more exciting, kind of life.

Then she had caught a bug and missed a party. Mark had gone along without her and met an exotic, half-Spanish girl there — who'd lured him away with scarcely any effort at all . . .

Now, her feet were just beginning to get used to the feel of solid earth again. But the memory of Mark's kisses could still send a wave of longing and misery through her.

"I'm sorry, Audrey, dear . . . We must talk when I get back. You're getting as bad as Dad for keeping things to yourself," Evelyn chided gently.

AT the station Liz came flying down the platform to greet her. She had inherited Ted's fair complexion and the sparkling eyes of her mother and Audrey, and she had a youthful beauty all of her own. "Audrey! And about time, too!" Liz cried, embracing her exuberantly. She was still slender, but rounded now and — outwardly, at least — a young woman.

"Let me take your bags. William's waiting outside, with transport."

"William?"

"There, you see! You're all out of touch. William lives next door — Mr Emmet retired and went to the coast.

"He's been an absolute gem with vital repairs," Liz went on breathlessly. "Remember that damp patch on the spare room wall? William not only tracked down the leak, he went up there and mended it.

"He's great!"

So much of William in the first two minutes! This, then, must be the young man of Evelyn's doubts . . .

An old van was parked by the station exit. Audrey had the impression of broad shoulders and brown hair, before 'William' turned and smiled — and gave her quite a shock.

This was no youth, but a fully-grown man.

Audrey supposed that William being around the house had thrown the two together, and Evelyn hadn't seen which way the wind was blowing until it was too late.

"Hello there," William said lazily, leaning over to open the door.

Audrey climbed in and Liz scrambled after her.

"I've been telling Audrey how useful you are," she informed him.

William grinned at Audrey through the driving mirror; a youthful, rakish grin. "And I sing 'Figaro' in the bath, too."

"We can hear him when the wind's in the right direction," Liz giggled.

"Will you eat with us tonight, William?" she added.

"Sorry. Have to put in a few extra hours at the shop."

"But you will be free next week, won't you? It's my party on Friday."

"I'll be around, never fear," William promised, dropping them at their adjoining gates.

"You didn't have much to say to William," Liz remarked, ushering Audrey into the cosy living-room. "You did like him, didn't you?"

"I had ample time to observe his charm," Audrey said drily. "But as for conversation, you did rather have the monopoly."

"Well, you know me — I always talk too much when I'm excited." She looked at her aunt a little uncertainly.

"You are all right, aren't you, Audrey? What with — Mark and . . .? You don't sound quite yourself."

"I'm fine." Hastily, Audrey smiled. She didn't want questions about Mark, and she'd certainly have to be more subtle about William.

"Good, because it's all hands on deck for my party . . .

"How d'you fancy making costumes? I'm hopeless at sewing."

"It's not fancy dress, is it?"

"It's Hallowe'en, remember? Witches and other ghoulish characters are the order of the evening. Broomsticks to be parked in the yard and we bob for apples by the light of turnip lanterns . . .!" Liz giggled, sounding more like last year's tomboy.

"Trouble is, I've never made a turnip lantern, have you?"

"No, but it shouldn't be too difficult."

"Oh well, we'll ask William. He's sure to know how.

"If you want to scuttle off and wash, I'll dish up supper. You're in the usual room — but note the new, unstained wallpaper!"

And I'll bet William put it on, Audrey thought drily.

She slept late, waking to a bright Saturday morning as Liz elbowed her way in with a breakfast tray. Today, with her hair tied in bunches, she looked about 12 years old.

"Special treat and don't drop your eggy soldiers on the pillows or Mum will stop our pocket money!"

Liz drank coffee, sitting cross-legged at the foot of the bed.

"I thought we'd do some shopping this morning. We can look round the market for party things.

"William will fetch the turnips in his car, but he's at his DIY shop today. He owns it, do you realise? Well, him and his bank manager between them do, as he says . . .

"As for our costumes — Mum said there's an old velvet frock in her wardrobe you can use. She can't get into it, so we can jazz it up with silver stars or something.

"And there's a black jumble-sale dress we can hack about for me."

The day passed swiftly and pleasantly. There was only the odd mention of William, Audrey noted — and no sign of him, until about 5.30, when the van drew up at the gate.

William came straight in after only the most perfunctory rap.

Audrey was standing on a chair in the medieval-styled velvet dress, while

Liz clumsily pinned on stars. "I'm coming as the hunchback of Notre Dame," he told them, after admiring the effect.

"But I was wondering what you're doing tonight? I heard there's a 'Son et Lumière' at the manor at half-eight, if you're interested. Have you been there, Audrey?"

"I went over the house years ago."

"Magnificent, isn't it? Well, I'll pick you both up around eight-fifteen, then — OK? Wrap up, we'll be sitting outside."

"Does he always dictate like that?" Audrey enquired when he'd gone.

Liz looked astonished.

"Dictate? You're not getting an attack of the middle ages along with this dress, are you? Wanting to consult your engagement book and book seats six months in advance?"

Audrey bit her tongue. She was going about discouraging Liz's interest in William in entirely the wrong way.

The evening was mild at first.

What with the special lights and sound effects, and the pageantry, Audrey found herself quite caught up in an atmosphere of an age gone by. William had brought along extra car rugs and, as the night got colder, put an arm round Liz, who was shivering. Liz snuggled close to him.

What on earth could she do, without appearing all prim and prudish, Audrey thought helplessly.

Next morning, Liz brought in mugs of tea and flung Audrey's window wide.

"Listen — can you hear him?"

"Hear who?" As if she couldn't guess!

"William, on the bells."

"*All* of them?" Audrey couldn't help murmuring. Was there no end to his accomplishments?

"Tell you what! I bet you've never seen bellringers at work, have you? Let's go to church early and watch them."

"Oh, Liz, no!"

"No? But — why ever not?"

"I — well — I'd hate anyone watching *me*."

"Oh, all right," Liz agreed disappointedly. "We probably couldn't prize Kath out of bed in time, anyway. Did I tell you we're calling for her on the way?"

Kathleen Gordon was Liz's best friend from her primary school days. While Audrey waited for her to find her coat, she could hear the girls talking.

"Guess what? The party list is down to unlucky thirteen!" Liz was saying triumphantly.

"Who's not coming?" Kathy enquired.

"The twins have to go away with the family, Mary's been invited out by some boy she's fancied for ages, and I'm passing up Bas. He got too big for his boots."

Great, Audrey thought wryly. Four fewer guests to distract her attention from William.

84

On Monday, Liz went off to school most reluctantly. Audrey was sweeping up leaves when William's head appeared over the adjoining wall.

"Hello there. Want a hand?"

"No, thanks," Audrey answered shortly. Obviously he was trying to curry the family's favour with all these odd jobs he kept doing.

"Are you sure?"

"Yes, really. I'm enjoying it."

"You have a garden yourself?"

"No. That's why I enjoy this one." She wielded the broom dismissively.

"Well — if you change your mind . . . Come over for elevenses later?"

"I'm going into town soon — I enjoy walking as well," she added hastily, forestalling offers of a lift.

$$\star \quad \star \quad \star \quad \star$$

That evening, Liz still seemed preoccupied by thoughts of the party — and William.

"I wonder if he collected the turnips," she said after supper. "I'll go and see, then we can make a start on the lanterns."

"Hadn't you better do your homework first, Liz?"

Liz paused halfway to the door, looking startled.

"For a minute, you sounded just like Mum!" She twitched her shoulders.

"I'd do anything to get out of it, you know. School, I mean," she muttered.

"Liz! But you're doing so well. You need qualifications to get on in the world nowadays —"

The words seemed like a spark to dry tinder.

"But I don't *want* to go to university and swot away to get letters after my name!

"Mum's so set on me having a career she thinks Dad would have been proud of, I just can't get through to her!" Two red spots burned on Liz's cheekbones.

"Sometimes I wish I hadn't slogged so hard to pass my exams — it only convinced Mum I'm cleverer than I am! What I really like is being — well — domestic.

"I love looking after Kath's kid brothers — and as for babysitting for pocket money, I feel guilty taking it! I can't think of anything more marvellous than having kids of your own . . ."

She glanced away, staring passionately out of the window, which looked out on William's house.

"And I don't suppose you know what I'm talking about, either!" she added, bitter with misery.

"But I do!" Audrey assured her quickly. "Only I think —"

"Then couldn't you talk to Mum?" she pleaded hopefully. "Tell her it's pointless for me to stay on —"

"But I'm not so sure I don't agree with her — up to a point, anyway!"

There were arguments churning in her head about youth and freedom, the need to live a little and gain experience before leaving the confines of school for those of marriage and motherhood, but she couldn't seem to marshal them in order.

"Liz, let's talk it out —" she begged, but Liz's face had closed up.

"There's no point. Even *you* don't understand . . . Oh, why can't anybody see I'm old enough now to know what I want?"

IZ was quiet over breakfast and, with the dismayed feeling that something warm and close between them had gone for good, Audrey didn't warm to William when he turned up in the afternoon with a bulging bag.

"I thought you'd be at the shop," she said unwelcomingly.

"I took a few days off — been working like a slave lately. How about these?"

He opened the bag and took out a large pumpkin and several outsized turnips, hollowed out and with nose and eye holes and grinning mouths.

"Shall we finish them off and set them in a row on the sideboard, ready for when Liz comes home?"

She stared at him, hardly hearing what he said. If Liz wouldn't see sense, perhaps she could get through to William . . .

Surely he'd want what was best for her, if he cared about her? But, where to start?

She plunged in before she lost her courage.

"William — how old are you?"

He looked mildly surprised.

"Thirty. Does it matter? My teeth are still my own and I can touch my toes without puffing."

His lazy grin gave her the impetus she needed.

"It's no joking matter!" she said angrily. "You're nearly twice Liz's age! You've turned her head and got her involved with emotions she's not old enough to cope with! Where's your sense of responsibility?"

"Liz?" he repeated blankly.

"Yes — Liz! Don't tell me you haven't noticed she's for ever at your heels! Her every other word is 'William'!"

E sat staring, his mouth open, and Audrey was assailed by a sudden awful doubt. For the first time, it occurred to her that William was not only innocent of encouragement, but also ignorant of the way Liz felt. "I've — I've put my foot in it, haven't I?" she said painfully, scarlet with embarrassment.

William seemed to make a great effort to find his voice. "But you must be mistaken! Liz is still a child!"

"You haven't been using your eyes, William," Audrey told him drily. "Evelyn was worried enough to mention it to me. She asked me to try to put a brake on Liz, but Liz won't listen to me either."

He looked at her closely.

"Is that why you've been giving me the cold shoulder?" he asked slowly. "You want me to keep away from Liz?"

Audrey's blush deepened.

"It's only . . . it's for Liz's good."

He frowned heavily and stood up.

"I wish Evelyn had . . ." He pushed a hand through his hair impatiently. "You've completely floored me, Audrey.

"OK, I'll melt away. Perhaps I shouldn't come to the party — unless seeing me alongside her own generation might be usefully off-putting . . .

"Oh, it all seems utterly ludicrous! I really can't . . ." He shook his head as if to clear it, and departed abruptly, in mid-sentence.

Audrey put her head in her hands. "It's all very well for *you*," she muttered at the grinning pumpkin.

AUDREY worked doubly hard at the party preparations to make up for William's absence. Liz seemed to have recovered her spirits and put aside her problem in the excitement of Hallowe'en. Friday came. They draped the buffet table with black crêpe paper, filled a water tub with rosy apples for bobbing and the air soon filled with the smell of delicious things heating in the oven.

"Funny William hasn't been round. There's been no sign of him for days," Liz commented, puzzled. "Perhaps the shop is giving him problems."

Kathy came early to help with last-minute touches. "I hope spirits won't get too high," Audrey murmured, while Liz was out of the room.

"It won't get out of hand," Kathy assured her. "Though it might have been another story if Bas was coming."

"Bas?"

"Yes — Basil Tillyer. Liz met him at a disco and had a real crush on him for a while. But they had a row the day before you came.

"I never liked him much, but he was twenty-one and very good-looking. I suppose Liz was flattered."

Audrey's legs began to shake.

What had she done? Why on earth hadn't Evelyn mentioned the boy's name and saved her all this!

William . . . well, she'd obviously misread Liz's natural fondness for a kindly neighbour who, maybe, had even helped to fill the gap left by her father . . .

"Actually I did want to speak to you about something else," Kathy was saying hesitantly.

"I know it's not really my business but — but Liz was terribly upset because you weren't for her idea of being a nanny.

"I know it's not the kind of highly-qualified job Mrs Hollins would like for Liz, but it is worthwhile, don't you think?" she pleaded earnestly.

"A nanny? But I don't recall Liz actually saying . . . She just went on about families and children."

Kathy shrugged.

"She's been so stewed up about it, not wanting to go against her mother, that —"

"I'll talk to her again," Audrey managed, her thoughts in turmoil. "I think there was a — a misunderstanding."

She felt such an idiot.

At nine o'clock, William still hadn't put in an appearance.

Liz seemed happy, though. At least for now.

"Come on, Audrey, you have to take a turn at this! Peel this apple all in one, then throw the peel over your left shoulder. It'll make the initial of your true love's name!"

Relieved at her party mood, Audrey took the fruit with a smile.

The peel fell into the rough shape of an M.

M for Mark, Audrey thought with a little shock. She hadn't given him a thought for days . . .

"It's a W!" Liz cried excitedly, viewing the peel from the other side.

As if on cue, the door opened and William walked in. Fortunately, his hunchback costume was so hideous that it took everyone's mind off Audrey's confusion.

But as soon as she could, Audrey sought him out alone.

"William — I made a mistake," she blurted, all her planned, dignified apologies gone to pot.

"I know," he said simply, glancing at her from beneath his eyebrows.

"When I thought about it — apart from the sheer unlikelihood of it all — I remembered something else," he explained. "From the time she knew you were coming, Liz's every other word to me has been 'Audrey'."

His eyes gleamed with amusement.

"I began to get faintly fed up with this paragon of an aunt . . . until I met her."

"Liz — match-making!" Audrey gasped indignantly. Then, when his last words sank in, she blushed. "Just wait — !"

"Don't be hard on her, she had your interests at heart. She was all het up about the recent man in your life making you unhappy —" He broke off. "Sorry. I'm speaking out of turn."

"No more than I did," she admitted.

And Liz has a point, she thought to herself.

"Coming to bob for apples, you two?" 'Cupid' called over.

William smiled at Audrey — a very telling smile that even transcended his hideous disguise . . . ∎

While her mum was simply trying to boost her confidence, another member of the family was working out a plan to blast it into orbit!

BELIEVE IN YOURSELF!

by Teresa Ashby

J AMIE was sick and tired of watching his older sister moping around the house. She seemed to spend her whole life in her bedroom, listening to slushy records or curled up with a romantic novel. It wasn't right for a girl of her age to be stuck indoors all the time. Susan was 19 — only five years older than Jamie.

Her only problem was acute shyness. She turned the colour of a ripe tomato if a man so much as *looked* at her.

And if she arranged a date with anyone, she got such a bad case of the jitters that she ended up taking to her bed and claiming to have caught Amazonian flu.

Her mother did everything she could to help. They went shopping for fashionable clothes, jewellery, make-up, all to boost Susan's confidence. And all to no avail.

"I'd be more confident if I was pretty," Jamie heard her complaining one day to their mother after one such bout of flu. "I know I would."

Jamie paused in the hall and listened at the half-open door.

"But you *are* pretty," their mother said. Jamie nodded silently to himself. He did think she was pretty.

She seemed to think that you had to look like Jerry Hall or something before anyone thought you were attractive. Jamie didn't care much for Jerry Hall, himself.

"No, I'm not," she said softly.

He peered round the door and saw the faint beginnings of a blush. She always blushed the reddest when someone paid her a compliment, even if it was a member of her own family.

"You are, Susan," their mother insisted tiredly.

She'd had this conversation 91 times, Jamie decided, yet still Susan wouldn't believe her.

"I've got a spot." She poked at a tiny pink blemish near her ear. "And . . . and my hair's just a mess."

"It's not a mess. It's thick and glossy. People pay a lot of money to get their hair looking like yours."

Jamie turned around and looked at his own reflection in the hall mirror.

"Like mine," he whispered, running his fingers through his blond curls.

"And . . . and my nose! It's a peculiar shape . . . see?" she turned side on and stuck her nose out.

"And I'm getting fat." She prodded her stomach.

"You're not fat." Mr Hetherington sighed and looked over the top of his newspaper. "There's nothing on you, my girl. Why . . . you're just a slip of a thing. Don't you dare start another diet!"

There was a short, stunned silence.

"There! See!" Susan cried triumphantly. "I'm much too skinny. Dad said so."

Jamie, still peering round the door, caught his father's eyes and they exchanged looks of male exasperation.

Looks they were exchanging more and more as Jamie grew older and less able to understand the opposite sex.

Women! There was just no pleasing them.

He turned back into the hall and scratched his chin. It was high time someone took Susan in hand!

And who better to do it than her brilliant, good-looking, never-stuck-for-an-idea and charmingly-modest-with-it, brother?

When confidence was handed out, Jamie had taken his sister's share as well as his own.

Already a fantastic plan was formulating in his mind.

It hadn't escaped Jamie's notice that the man at No. 42 had captured Susan's interest.

Alan Carter seemed to have a similar problem to her, though. If ever they met face to face, he tended to reflect Susan's colour.

They had never managed more than a garbled, "Good morning," on the two or three occasions they'd actually met.

But, Jamie had caught Susan leaning out of her bedroom window just to watch Alan washing his car.

And he'd seen him, too, watching her with dreamy eyes as she chugged up the road on her moped, going to work at the local library.

Yes, there was certainly something there worth building on . . .

The trouble with his wonderful idea was that he needed someone else's co-operation. Somehow, though, he couldn't see his parents ever agreeing to what he had in mind.

Auntie Grace was possible, though. She was always trying to persuade Susan to go out more. But it would really need to be someone who wouldn't tell Susan.

Salvation came in the form of Damson from No. 35. She was in his class at school and everyone liked her. She was so clever and sophisticated.

If only Susan had just half her confidence . . . Jamie sighed.

Damson's parents were very fond of fruit.

They had two other children, Kiwi and Robin. They had lost interest in fruit after Kiwi was born and had taken up bird-watching just before their son was born.

They were hot on potted plants at the moment and expecting another baby. Jamie often wondered what that poor little soul would be called.

Polyanthus perhaps, or maybe Yucca . . .

ANYWAY, when Jamie approached Damson with his plan, she was only too willing to help. She sat down immediately to write the two letters. She was really marvellous at writing letters and provided no end of sick notes and excuse-mes for her friends. She'd helped Jamie get a few days off to watch some of the Wimbledon matches in July, so he knew she could do it. She picked up her pen, they put their heads together and she began to write.

Dear Miss . . .

"No, no, put Ms," Jamie said. "Go on, or else she'll think he's an old fogey."

Damson looked doubtful, but obligingly screwed up the paper and began again on another sheet of paper.

Dear Mz Hetherington . . .

"Perhaps Dear Susan would be better," Jamie suggested.

Damson sighed.

"Who is writing this letter?"

"You are."

"Right."

Dear Mz Hetherington,

I hear it is your birthday and it would give me the utmost pleasure . . .

"Hang on," Jamie said. "Isn't it a bit . . ."

He laughed nervously as Damson pressed her lips hard together.

"No . . . no never mind," he said. "It's just right. Carry on, Damson."

. . . if you would do me the honour of coming out with me for a celebrashun. I will call for you at seven o'clock. Yours truly, Mr Alan Carter.

They both smiled in satisfaction and Damson reached for another sheet of paper.

Dear Mr Carter,

I have admired you from afar and as next Friday is my birthday I would be honoured for you to join me in a special celebrashun. I will leave the choice of a venyou to you. Yours sincerely, Mz Susan Hetherington.

"There." Damson folded both letters neatly and slipped them into their envelopes. "I'll deliver Mr Carter's. I like him, he's nice."

"OK," Jamie agreed. Damson was a good sort, he thought. It was almost a pity she wasn't a boy. Then they could have been *real* friends.

"I'll give my sister hers on Tuesday," he went on. "That way she won't have too much time to come down with Amazonian flu."

"I hope it works, Jamie, really I do," Damson said kindly. "I think your sister is ever so nice and so's Mr Carter. They'd make a lovely couple."

"I hope it works, too," Jamie said sincerely.

If it didn't work and his family ever found out that he'd been behind it, they'd never forgive him.

Jamie could hardly wait for Susan's birthday to come around.

She was the only person he knew who'd once hidden under the table when her birthday cake was carried in. That was when she was a child, though. Yet he could remember sitting in his high chair all those years ago, and blowing out her candles for her.

Funny, but *she* still got the wish.

It got so bad that Mrs Hetherington gave up having parties for her daughter. Since then her birthdays had always passed by very peacefully.

Auntie Grace did her best, bless her heart, to bring Susan out of her shell.

One year, she bought her a kite, a really flashy one all the way from Japan. But Susan insisted on flying it in their back garden.

Now, the moped had been a brilliant flash of inspiration on Auntie's part (again from Japan). Except that Susan used it in order to *avoid* other people.

FRIDAY saw Susan, blushing like a faulty traffic light, accepting her presents with shy thank-yous. She loved the new clothes from her parents and she liked the perfume (guaranteed to attract men or your money back) from Auntie Grace.

But Jamie's present, as always, was the best.

Susan was thrilled with the manicure set. She said she'd put it in the drawer with all the others.

Then the big moment came and he handed her the note.

"This, er, came through the door," he said nonchalantly, "while you were opening your presents."

"A letter?" She blushed. "For me?"

She tore it open with trembling fingers and if it was possible, she went two shades redder.

"It's . . . it's from Alan Carter," she stammered. "He wants to take me out tonight for a . . . oh dear, the poor man. For a birthday treat, he says."

"And you'll go too, my girl," Mrs Hetherington said firmly. "You've been going on about him for weeks and I'm not going to stand by and see you pass up this opportunity."

Jamie was beside himself with excitement. It looked like his plan would work. There wasn't time for Susan to develop flu symptoms — not even of the notoriously-fast-acting variety.

Even if she had, Auntie Grace and his mother would have seen to it that she recovered quickly.

Even Jamie was amazed at how eagerly she prepared for her date that evening.

As soon as she got home from work she put on a face pack, spent an hour and a half in the bath and went through all her clothes.

It was a treat to see. Auntie Grace said it was quite a turn up for the books, then took herself off to the bingo, grinning happily to herself.

THE magic hour arrived at last. Seven o'clock. Mr and Mrs Hetherington sat twiddling their thumbs and Jamie sat on the chair under the window, pretending to read an electronics book. But in reality every nerve was stretched to hear the first sounds of Alan Carter arriving.

Susan was probably blushing, but it was impossible to see because she'd bought herself some special green make-up to hide it.

Actually, Jamie thought she looked awful. Not at all like Susan. With her solid chalky face (she looked like a vampire) and her dark, terrified eyes peering out, he hardly knew her.

She kept going on and on about it being such a shame that grown-up people were unable to spell or write properly and how she would like to make it her mission in life to help at least one other adult to learn to spell.

Ten past seven and no sign of Alan Carter.

You could have cut the atmosphere with a knife.

Susan had started to pick at her nail varnish and Mr Hetherington was wobbling his pipe from one side of his mouth to the other.

Mrs Hetherington had arranged and rearranged the cushions half a dozen times and had now started polishing the television screen.

Jamie tried to look as though he was concentrating on his book. He doodled in the margin with a pencil, writing his name. Beside it, he wrote, "Damson" then he scored it out.

What had gone wrong? Surely Damson remembered to deliver the note?

Half-past seven and it was obvious that Alan Carter had stood Susan up. She was stricken.

"I'm going to have a bath," she said, scowling so hard that she nearly cracked her make-up. "And then I'm going to bed. I can't be bothered with people who were probably delinquents at school."

"He's most likely been delayed, dear," Mrs Hetherington said sympathetically. "Maybe you should telephone . . ."

"Telephone? Him?" she spluttered. "Not on your life. Don't you see, it's just a joke. He's just trying to make a fool of me."

"No, it can't be a joke," Jamie said quickly. "He's not that sort of guy. He likes you, Susan, I'm sure he does!"

His voice held a desperate note and he swallowed nervously.

Susan gave him a withering look. "He likes me so much he keeps me waiting around like this?"

"But you can't have a bath," Jamie cried, hoping against hope that Alan Carter would still arrive. "You've already had a bath. You were in it for hours!"

She made a noise which sounded halfway between a groan and a scream and ran upstairs.

"Oh dear," Mr Hetherington said.

"Poor Susan." His wife shook her head sadly. "Nothing ever goes right for her, does it?"

JAMIE crept into the hall and picked up the telephone. Damson was racked with guilt. She didn't know how it had happened. She couldn't imagine what made her forget. "I'll take it round to him straightaway," she offered.

"It's too late," Jamie said miserably.

Things were worse now than before. Damson had let them down and between them they'd probably ruined Susan's whole life.

He was still mooning around in the hall when the doorbell rang less than 15 minutes later.

"I'll get it," he said. It was probably Auntie Grace, so loaded down with winnings that she couldn't get her key out.

Susan was still in the bath. He could hear the occasional splash and angry yells and guessed she was drowning the rubber ducks.

She could be very violent if things didn't go her way . . .

Alan Carter was standing on the doorstep, a bunch of flowers (which looked suspiciously like Mr Smith's treasured pink roses) clasped in his hand.

"Is Susan ready?" he enquired.

Before Jamie could reply, his mother had come storming into the hall.

"You've got a nerve, young man, turning up here nearly an hour late and expecting Susan to be ready," she said angrily.

"I'm terribly sorry, Mrs Hetherington," Alan said. "But I didn't receive Susan's note until a few minutes ago."

He turned to look accusingly at Jamie.

"Perhaps someone forgot to deliver it."

"*Susan's* note?" Mrs Hetherington said.

Jamie crept upstairs and knocked on the bathroom door. He didn't want to be around when the truth came out. As it inevitably would.

"Are you out of the bath yet, Susan?" he asked.

"Yes," she called back. At least she sounded calm now. He couldn't hear any rubber ducks hitting the door or sponges thumping the walls.

"Will you be down soon?" Jamie said. He hoped she'd protect him, but deep down he knew that she'd probably be the one to kill him.

"Soon. Tell Mum I'll make coffee when I come down."

"Great." Jamie nodded to himself, then went back downstairs.

It was like the Inquisition downstairs. All three of them were sitting in the front room with poker faces.

Alan was still hanging on grimly to his flowers. Mr Hetherington was gnawing on his pipe and Mrs Hetherington had started on the cushions again.

"What do you know about this?" Mr Hetherington said sternly. "Was this your idea of a practical joke?"

There were only two ways out. He could deny everything, or he could blame Damson. He looked at Alan.

Alan didn't look quite so mad. His eyes were twinkling and there was a hint of a smile at the corners of his mouth.

"I only wanted to help," Jamie blurted, staring at the coffee stain which was supposed to be hidden beneath the waste-paper basket.

"You've put Susan — and Alan — into a very embarrassing situation," Mr Hetherington went on. "I think the very least you can do is apologise."

"I should go and . ." Mrs Hetherington began, but stopped mid-sentence, her mouth dropping open as she stared in horror at her daughter now standing in the doorway.

SHE was wearing her old dressing-gown and had a ghastly, bright-orange towel wrapped, turban-like, around her head. She'd scrubbed all the make-up off as well and looked, Jamie thought, much prettier. Alan stood up and dropped the flowers. He went very red.

"You look lovely," he said, oblivious to everyone else in the room. Mrs Hetherington looked as if she'd enjoy wringing her son's neck.

"I do?" Susan stammered, turning pink.

"So natural . . . I've always admired the way you look so natural."

"You have?"

"Look, I'm terribly sorry I'm late." He licked his lips nervously and glanced towards the Hetheringtons who were all watching him intently.

"I . . . I was unavoidably detained . . . yes, that's what happened . . .

"I . . . my car broke down and I couldn't get to a phone. I wouldn't have let you down for the world, so . . . would you still like to come out?"

You couldn't see Susan for dust. Upstairs, there were all the normal, frantic sounds of an older sister getting ready for a date.

The hairdryer was whirring and wardrobe doors were slamming as she went through the performance of finding something to wear all over again.

When they'd finally gone, (glowing pinkly, both of them) Mr Hetherington turned on his son.

"That was a near disaster," he said.

"Yes, but it turned out all right, didn't it?" Jamie retorted proudly. He was delighted with the way things had gone.

He'd never seen his sister looking so pleased with herself and he'd even detected a faint whiff of Auntie Grace's perfume as she swept out of the door.

"No thanks to you," Mr Hetherington observed drily. "If young Carter there hadn't been such a gentleman, it could have been very embarrassing for your sister. Very embarrassing indeed.

"As it is, we've agreed that Susan need never know about your joke.

"Who did write the letters, anyway? I'd have known your spider's crawl."

"Damson," Jamie admitted sheepishly. He wasn't sure he liked his father's remark about his writing being a spider's crawl. He did his best, for goodness' sake!

"Then you'd better have a word with young Damson and make sure she keeps it a secret, too.

"And if she's going to make a habit of writing letters like that, she'd better get herself a dictionary. Her spelling is awful."

THE following morning, Jamie asked his starry-eyed sister if she wanted to come swimming as they normally did on Saturdays. Susan shook her head regretfully. "I'm sorry, Jamie, I forgot all about that and Alan's taking me out. But I'll be glad to come along another time." She slipped five pounds into her brother's hand.

"I'm sure you'll be able to think of someone to take with you if you want to," she winked.

Jamie had never seen his sister wink before!

Then she hugged and kissed him.

It was a very disgruntled and disillusioned Jamie that went round to call on Damson.

"How did it go?" she said eagerly. "I took the letter round. Did he turn up?"

"Yes he did but we've got to keep it a secret from Susan. She'd die if she found out, apparently. Well, that's what my dad said and Auntie Grace said that I'd die if Susan found out.

"You can keep a secret, can't you, Damson?"

"Of course I can."

"That's it then, thanks for your help." Jamie turned around and thrust his hands into his pockets. Then he had another bright idea.

"Hey, Damson," he said, swinging round, "I don't suppose you'd like to come swimming this afternoon, would you? I'll pay."

Damson's eyes lit up.

"I'd love to, Jamie," she said, smiling. "Thanks for asking me."

"Great." Jamie rubbed his hands together. Now he wasn't going to have to accompany his sister everywhere, he could start having fun.

He hadn't thought of that before. And looking at Damson, he was all of a sudden very glad she wasn't a boy. Because somehow that meant they could be real friends, after all. ■

World Of Our Own

They'd planned their future together. So why, now, did she feel so isolated and alone?

by Isobel Stewart

THE little room, the room that was waiting for the baby, was perfect. Winter sunlight shone through the lemon-sprigged curtains and gleamed on the white nursery furniture, the mobile hanging above the cot, the cheerful frieze of animals.

In the cupboard, neatly stacked, were piles of nappies, tiny vests, miniature bootees.

The baby wasn't due for almost two months, but as soon as she stopped work, Sue had started planning and organising. Now everything was ready for the baby.

Everything, Sue thought, with sudden and shattering clarity, except me.

In the silence of the small room, it seemed, for a moment, as if she had said the words aloud, as if they hung there in the air, accusingly.

But of course she had only thought them and it was such a foolish thought that she certainly wasn't going to dwell on it — she'd force herself to forget about it.

After all, this baby was wanted and planned. Three years, they'd said they would wait.

Three years of being free, of doing what they wanted when they wanted, of being just the two of them, and then it would be the right time to start a family.

And everything had gone exactly as they'd planned.

Sue sat down in the rocking-chair. Brian had bought it as soon as they knew she was pregnant, scraped it down and painted it white, and she had made a cushion for it. She would sit in it when she fed the baby, she had told him, placing the chair where she would be able to look out the window.

And as she said it, she'd had a picture of herself nursing her baby, calmly, serenely, tranquilly.

She began to rock, gently, determinedly trying to will herself into that Sue — the Sue who should already be calm and serene and tranquil as she waited for her baby.

But I'm not any of these things, she thought slowly, painfully and honestly.

I'm restless, I'm bored at home, I don't like the way I look, often I don't like the way I feel. And — I'm not too sure that I'm going to like things any better when the baby is actually here.

Now there was no pushing the thought away, now she had to face it. It had been there, deep down, she admitted, for some time. Weeks? Months? Sue honestly didn't know.

It was difficult now, to look back and try to recapture how she'd felt at the beginning. Surprised, most of all, she thought, that the baby had been on the way almost as soon as they'd decided it was time.

Surely, she thought guiltily, she'd been thrilled as soon as she knew for certain. Surely?

And Brian? How did he really feel? He didn't talk very much about the baby, but she hadn't expected him to.

He'd painted her chair for her, put up shelves in the nursery, and been very involved in the choosing of the pram and the cot.

But these were practical things and Brian was a practical man. Surely these things meant that he wanted the baby, that he was looking forward to them being a family?

Or did they just mean that Brian, too, was in the situation of being a father-to-be and he was making the best of it? She should ask him, Sue knew that.

They'd always talked about things that either of them saw as a problem. A problem? Once again, she was taken aback by the direction of her thoughts. A problem — the baby they had planned?

We should talk about it, Sue told herself. But she wasn't sure if she could handle finding out that Brian, too, had reservations about the baby.

The phone rang, startling her, and she managed to rise clumsily, annoyed at her own awkwardness.

It was Julie, one of her friends from the office.

"Sue? How's it going? Two months to go, isn't it?" And hardly waiting for an answer, she hurried on breathlessly, "I've got to be quick, Mr Payne is going to ring for me for dictation any minute, but listen, we're having a party tonight.

"It's to celebrate New Year. Can you and Brian come? Bring some wine and if you really feel like it, do one of your delicious garlic loaves. Around eight — all right?"

A moment later Sue put the phone down, feeling as breathless as Julie had sounded, having agreed to go to the party and take the garlic loaf.

And as she turned away, she had a sudden pang of pure envy as she pictured Julie rising from her desk, her long, blonde hair swinging, her skirt slim and smooth, hurrying through to Mr Payne's office, her eyebrows rising expressively to the other girls as she went.

A party, how lovely, she told herself brightly, and suddenly the whole day had an aim and a point to it.

She would have to wash her hair, she decided, and buy a loaf from the corner shop. If she walked down now, that would be her usual daily walk.

The day passed more quickly and more pleasantly than usual, she thought, a little guiltily.

Before she knew it, Brian was home and they were having a snack and discussing the evening ahead. "What are you wearing, love?" Brian asked. "My loose cotton dress," she told him. "It accommodates both of us quite nicely."

"I like it," he said a little abstractedly, and he held out his mug for more coffee. "How was your day?"

"Fine," she replied, perhaps a little too quickly, for she found his eyes resting on her questioningly.

For a moment she had a longing to burst into tears and to tell him all the things she'd been thinking, all the things she'd been feeling.

But that might open the door for Brian to agree with her, to admit that he wasn't too sure if he felt ready for the baby — and she didn't want that tonight — not when they were going to a party.

"I'm looking forward to the party," she said, rinsing her mug at the sink. "We haven't done anything like this for ages — we seem to have been out of touch."

"I suppose we have," Brian agreed. He rinsed his mug, too, and followed her through to the bedroom.

"Now that these last bank exams are over we can get back in touch with everything — do a bit more, get around a bit more. We might as well, while we can."

"While we can," Sue agreed, hoping her words didn't sound as hollow on the outside as they felt on the inside.

The loose cotton dress was creamy white and so flattering that she'd loved it the moment she'd seen it. It made her skin look clear, and it did something to the colour of her hair.

I look quite nice, Sue thought, studiously avoiding the bulge of her tummy as she inspected her reflection in the mirror. And then, with determination — I look very nice. The jacket disguises my shape.

"This is going to be fun," she said to Brian as they went in the open door of Julie's flat. "Julie's parties always are."

THE party was already going well. In one room, all the furniture had been pushed to the wall to leave some space for dancing, and in the other, people were sitting on big cushions on the floor, talking. Julie's circle had changed somewhat, Sue realised, as she looked around for familiar faces.

There were plenty of people they knew but there were undoubtedly some new folk here.

Two or three times, as they made their way through the room where the dancing was, they stopped to talk, above the music, to people they knew, and just at the far end, Julie reached them.

"Hi, Brian — Sue," she said, loudly, above the music. "Sue, you look marvellous. But hey — are you sure it isn't twins?"

"Actually, I haven't put on very much weight," Sue replied a little stiffly, but Julie wasn't really listening.

"Come in and sit down — look, there's space beside Margie and Ted," she said.

The accepted thing for parties like this was big cushions on the floor. Everyone did it. We used to do it, too, Sue thought.

She looked down at the large cushion beside Margie and she knew that there was no way she could get down there and sit without looking very clumsy, very awkward and very, very pregnant.

She looked at Brian.

"I can't sit on the floor," she said flatly.

"I'll get you a chair," he said, and in a moment he had found one and helped her to move the cushion and sit down.

"I said, how do you feel, Sue?" Margie asked, and Sue bent down to reply, to say that she felt fine, thank you.

"Another year and that will be me," Margie said cheerfully. "We just want this holiday on the Continent first, then next year will be Baby Year.

"You two can give us lots of advice by then, I'm sure." She scrambled easily to her feet and held out one hand to her husband, Ted.

"They've put on our record, we just have to dance — come on, Ted."

She looked at Brian. He was talking to Phil and he didn't seem to realise it was a Beatles record.

"Brian," she said loudly. "It's 'Yesterday'."

He looked at her.

"So it is, but are you sure you should?"

"Of course I'm sure," she replied.

They danced fairly sedately and then the music changed to 'Hard Day's Night.' Sue had always loved it and it was ages since they'd danced to it.

"Sue — be careful, love, take it easy," Brian said, close to her ear. He was smiling, but his eyes were anxious. "Remember the baby!"

She stopped. "Let's sit down," she said quietly.

He looked down at her. "We don't have to," he told her. "Just take it easy."

She shook her head. "I'd rather sit down," she said.

She sat down in her chair and looked around the room at the heads on a level with her knees.

I'm separate from all this, she thought. I'm not a part of it.

On one side, Margie and Ted were talking about the Greek Island part of the trip they were planning. On the other, two people she didn't know were telling a small group how they'd just sold everything they possessed and were going off to live in a kibbutz for a year.

"And after that we might go anywhere, do anything," the girl said excitedly.

"Food, everyone," Julie called. "Sit still, Sue, I'll bring you some. You're entitled to special treatment."

But I don't want this special treatment, Sue thought, sadly. I just want to be like everyone else.

"Thank you," she said politely, when Julie brought her a plate of moussaka.

"Your bread went so quickly I didn't even get a piece," Brian told her when he came back.

He looked at her. "You're tired, love," he said, and the concern in his voice brought a tightness to Sue's throat. "I think we should go home as soon as possible."

IT wasn't, of course, possible. Ted got out his guitar, and played, and then someone suggested making Irish coffees. Sue, looking at Brian, saw that he was quiet, remote. Remote, she thought, from the room, from the party and from her.

He minds, too, that we're not part of this any longer, she thought sadly. Perhaps he's also thinking that we're not really ready to have a baby.

He was quiet all the way home and she didn't really feel like saying very much. But when they were inside, he looked down at her and touched her cheek gently.

"Go to bed, love," he told her. "I'll bring you a cup of tea."

Obediently, Sue went upstairs. But at the top of the stairs she hesitated and then, not really knowing why she was doing it, she went into the baby's room.

It was dark and she switched on the little nightlight they had bought. The room looked different with the dim pool of light.

I've never been in here at night before, Sue thought. And then — but I will be, often. So many times, in the still of the night, I'll be in here.

She walked over to the cot and looked down into it. And then she touched the pram, tentatively, then the baby bath, set in its special table.

And then she sat down in her rocking-chair, her hands folded over the bulge that was the baby.

Late at night seemed to be the baby's time for activity and now there was a sudden vigorous kick.

In spite of herself, Sue smiled. Softly, she touched the place where the kick had been and it happened again.

"You didn't like the party too much either, then?" she said softly. And slowly, certainly, the party and the way she had felt took on a distance, a lack of importance.

She rocked gently, sitting there in the dimly-lit little room and the thoughts she'd had that morning and then again at the party, seemed absurd, unreal. Oh yes, she thought, with a certainty that warmed her entire body. Oh yes, my baby, I want you. I want you and I love you and I don't know why I felt so strange.

The baby inside her was so real now that she thought she could hardly wait these last two months. Her arms ached to hold it.

How could I have thought I wasn't ready, she asked herself, amazed.

And then, sobering her down, damping her inexplicable joy, came the thought of Brian. It wasn't enough that *she* was now ready for the baby . . .

She hadn't heard him come upstairs, but suddenly, softly, he was there, beside her.

"I wondered where you were," he said. "Are you all right?"

"Yes," she replied soberly. "I am now."

And it wasn't difficult, somehow, to tell him how she'd been feeling. After a little while, he knelt down beside her and put his arms around her, just holding her, and that helped even more.

It wasn't difficult then to say why she hadn't asked him how he felt about the baby.

"And then, the party," she said at last.

"Yes, the party," he agreed.

"I couldn't sit on the floor and I couldn't dance the way I wanted to and — and all the girls looked so slim and they talked about their holidays, and — I felt right out of it," she told him.

"And I looked at you, and you were so — remote — that I was sure you were thinking, too —"

She touched his head.

"What were you thinking, Brian?" she asked him steadily.

He looked up at her.

"I was thinking that we have moved on," he said, after a while. "We're the first of the people we know to get into the baby business."

Because there was something in his voice that told her, already, that it was all right, an irrepressible little giggle rose inside her.

"Not the baby business," she said softly. "Just one little baby."

For a moment his hand rested on the bulge.

"For starters," he agreed. "Just one little baby." And then he was serious again.

"Oh, Sue love, I've thought all the things you've thought. I've woken up at night, sometimes, and I've looked at you lying asleep there and I've wondered at myself, at the responsibility for you and now for the baby.

"And I've thought, too, that maybe we should have waited a little longer. But I don't really think that would have made much difference. In fact, in some ways I think it was easier years ago when people didn't have these years of freedom first.

"No, I think I would have been — sobered, at any time, by the thought. And the changes — you're so right there, everything is going to change for us.

"But remember, this is our baby, yours and mine. She might have eyes like yours, a smile like yours . . ."

"He," she said, not quite steadily. "He might have your nose — your chin —"

She put her arms around him and they held each other. "What made you feel differently?" he asked at last. "I don't know," she said slowly, honestly. "I came in here, and — the baby kicked — he often kicks late at night, but — he seemed to be making a comment on the party, on the stupid way I'd been feeling and — and I just knew that I was ready for him.

"In a way, that is much more important than all these things here in the room. They're fine and they're necessary, but — the way we feel matters much more."

Brian stood up and took both her hands, helping her to her feet.

"Time you were in bed," he told her. "You'd better have your tea and your digestive biscuit, for your heartburn."

His arms around her shoulders were warm, wrapping her in a blanket of loving and caring.

My digestive biscuit for my heartburn, she thought, sleepily, happily, and it was as if he had told her he had a dozen red roses waiting for her.

He switched off the little nightlight and the room was once again in darkness.

Waiting.

Waiting for the baby. ■

"LET'S CALL

The trouble with getting off to a bad start is that things are liable to get even worse . . .

by D.L. Garrard

SHOO!" I shouted. "Stay away from my cabbages!" The pigeon turned to regard me with round yellow eyes, but didn't move. I'd saved long and hard for this house. It had been in a bit of a mess, and the grounds had been a shambles. Having lived in a bachelor flat for so long, I was determined the garden would be my pride and joy. Getting that in order for the summer was my first priority.

But this pigeon nipping the tops of my seedlings wasn't helping at all.

I clapped my hands vigorously. "Go on — take your custom elsewhere."

"Croo!" the pigeon said disdainfully, and made for the tiny pea shoots pushing their way through the earth. I was furious. I'd hoped my garden would impress Gillian when she came for dinner on Sunday. Pretty, dainty Gillian who'd bowled me over the minute I'd laid eyes on her at a party a month ago.

Now, how was I to prove what an able provider I could be if my garden was ruined by one little pigeon?

"Be very careful," I muttered, stalking the bird, "or the main dish on Sunday night may be pigeon pie!" The pigeon pulled up another seedling.

"That does it!" I hurled a clod of earth, not quite at the pigeon but near enough to put it in a flutter.

But it only flapped as far as the fence and from there surveyed me with a cheeky look in its eye.

My next clod hit the top of the fence and the bird swooped into my pear tree, which overhung the next garden.

Next door had been empty for a long time, even before I moved in, but I'd heard from Mrs Robbins, a neighbour, that it was now sold. But I'd seen nobody around . . .

"What d'you think you're doing?"

The voice made me start.

A flushed female face appeared above the fence — and pierced me through with a sizzling stare. A thick plait of fair hair crowned her head, making her even taller. A sunburned hand removed a lump of dirt from the coronet.

"How dare you throw stones at that pigeon? You might have killed him!"

I smiled placatingly and somewhat nervously. I did not want to fall out with the neighbours, especially if they were Amazons.

"Oh, no, no. I wouldn't have killed him. I'm not the kind of person coconut-shy owners get wealthy on. I never hit anything. Except my thumb with a hammer."

A TRUCE..."

She gave me a withering look and called to the pigeon who was perching on a nearby branch. At her inviting chirrup it came to hop at her feet like a dog come to heel.

"You speak its language!" I observed, fascinated.

"He belonged to my uncle. He was a racing pigeon but he didn't make the grade."

"Too much stopping off *en route* to refuel?" I asked cheerfully. "Well, Percy Pigeon . . ."

"His name's Charlemagne."

That threw me for a moment, but in true style I soon gathered my wits.

"Mine's Harry Wade. And so long as *he* keeps his beady eyes off my French beans —"

"Birds will be birds. Try bits of paper to flap in the wind — or some old net curtains over your seedlings," she said casually, then added more directly, "I hope you aren't using sprays and things, they're harmful to wildlife."

She popped the pigeon into his roosting box, which was adjacent to her back porch, then went indoors still fishing bits of dirt out of her hair.

But I had no intention of conducting Gillian round a display of bird frighteners and old net curtains. I spent most of my free time pigeon watching. Charlemagne watched me just as assiduously, and did his pilfering when I took a break.

GILLIAN'S reaction to my domain was disappointing. Perhaps I shouldn't have kept the whole thing a surprise. She was wearing high heels and a flimsy frock which seemed to catch on every twig, bush and beanstick, and came completely to grief among the straggling old gooseberry bushes.

"You should clip them back off the path, Harry," she reproached with commendable restraint as I released her from their thorny embrace.

"I'm very sorry. I've been concentrating more on planting the vegetables. This is my compost heap," I announced proudly in a louder tone. "People take it for granted everyone uses chemicals, but I never touch the things."

The girl next door was up a ladder, stripping paint from an upstairs window. She wore black dungarees and a striped yellow and black T-shirt. From this angle she looked like a very tall wasp.

She heard me, as I'd intended, and gave me an ironic look at this late riposte.

"Pity you can't trot into the street with a shovel after the milkman's horse, like my granddad used to," she shouted down. "Marvellous for the roses, he always told me."

"Oh —hi," I said, wishing I'd held my tongue. "Meet Gillian. Gillian — er —"

"Pat Snow. Hello, Gillian."

"Hello," Gillian said politely. "Shall we go indoors?" she whispered to me. "I don't think I want to know about compost heaps and the milkman's horse just before dinner."

I'd intended to serve apéritifs outside, visualising Gillian's hand stealing into mine in the early summer evening. But what with the pungent smell of paint stripper, not to mention the curls of sticky old paint falling over my side of the fence, I didn't suggest it.

Pat Snow was whistling, too. A piercing, tuneless sound which set my teeth on edge.

"What do you think of my home, Gillian?"

"Well," she said, sipping her Martini. "Since you ask, Harry, it is a bit dark and poky. That's the trouble with these very old properties."

106

"I could knock out the centre wall, I suppose, and put in French windows," I said slowly. "But I don't want to spoil the atmosphere."

"There still wouldn't be room for modern furniture," Gillian said.

"I like all this old-fashioned stuff — especially the Welsh dresser."

"Well I prefer light, modern furniture myself. And really deep, upholstered easy chairs. Even the rocker's more wood than cushion, isn't it?"

The candles I'd lit attracted several fat moths and the dinner got cold while I knocked over the gravy in pursuit of them.

"Don't worry about it, Harry, I don't like eating big meals in the evening anyway."

When I suggested another date she smiled apologetically.

"Let's be honest with each other, Harry. It's not going to work. We just don't want the same things. Maybe we could just be good friends."

WHEN she'd gone I wandered outside, clutching the bottle of red wine by the neck. Gillian only drank white. She was right, though, there were a lot of things I'd been blind to. It was almost dark. Pat was backing carefully down the ladder.

"You must be thirsty after all that whistling. Care for some wine?"

"No, thanks. Not on an empty stomach."

"You're welcome to a slice of congealed lamb and I'm sure I could wring some gravy out of the tablecloth."

I took another swig. She reached over the fence and removed a dead moth from my breast pocket.

"Why don't you chuck that bottle in the bin and have a nice lie down? I think you've drunk too much of it, as it is."

"No fear. The wine isn't going to be wasted as well. Spoiled food *and* a broken relationship."

I was silent for a moment then went on.

"Your activities out here didn't help, you know."

I realised hazily that wasn't fair, but I didn't have time to repent. Pat glowered at me.

"Am I supposed to suspend my life for your benefit? It's debatable whether this house will fall down faster than I can shore it up!"

"You must have known what it was like when you bought it. If you thought you couldn't cope . . ."

"It was exactly what I wanted and could afford! And anyway . . ." She broke off abruptly as if she'd just remembered something, then ran off indoors. I heard a door slam, then another.

I looked up to make sure her chimney pot was still intact, then defiantly drained the bottle. I'd always thought I was a fairly easy-going fellow until I came across Pat Snow.

On Sunday I bumped into Mrs Robbins on the way back from the local paper shop. She invited me in for a quick cup of tea, which I felt forced to accept. Mrs Robbins makes the best fruit scones in town.

She also said she had something for me — well, for the house, she told me.

Since I'd arrived in the street she'd taken me under her wing, so to speak. I think she was convinced that a man alone just couldn't survive.

She waited until I was sitting back, comfortably replete, before dropping the surprise into my arms.

It was a bundle of rust-coloured spiky fur; everything about it stood on end. Its eyes were huge and astonished and even its whiskers looked surprised.

"One of my nieces presented it to me under the illusion that I'm a lonely old lady who needs a cat to love.

"She's rather sweet in spite of her odd appearance — the pussy-cat, I mean. But I often go away to stay with friends and I'm just the slightest bit sneezy when there's fur around.

"She'll be good in the garden, birds don't like a cat around. Nor do mice."

The kitten was rubbing the edge of her jaw, hard as iron, along the edge of my chin. Her whiskers pricked my nose and her tail, fuzzy as a bottle brush, poked in my ear. She vibrated visibly.

"She's an affectionate little thing, though a bit of a cowardy custard. What'll you call her, Harry? I never got around to naming her."

"Arabella," I said.

"How's your new neighbour getting on with her house repairs?" Mrs Robbins pursued.

I grunted. "She seems to be one of nature's handymen. Makes me feel quite inadequate,

"I'm not so sure. Her boyfriend wanted her to buy the place, you know. He was going to do it up for her."

"I didn't know that. I've seen no signs of a boyfriend."

Mrs Robbins gave the ladylike version of a sniff. "He left before you moved in. They were to get married after she came back from doing some voluntary service overseas, which she'd committed herself to. Only he found someone else.

"So Pat was left alone with that great white elephant of a place. I don't know how she copes, alone . . ."

For the first time, I began to wonder, too.

I buttered Arabella's paws but she didn't really need any inducement to stay. Like me, she felt quite at home in the big old-fashioned house and quickly made her presence felt.

She chose a low chair and told me where she wanted her saucer, then curled up for a long nap. She wouldn't have ventured out at all if I hadn't persuaded her with a firm push on her furry behind.

"It's only a little garden, you won't get lost. Get some fresh air and test your claws on the fence instead of that chair leg!"

Shortly afterwards I became aware of a thin, high-pitched screeching.

On investigating, I discovered the kitten had clawed her way up the fence and leapt over, landing more by luck than judgment on top of the pigeon roost.

She teetered there, claws dug into the roof, wailing like a banshee.

The pigeon was tripping back and forth making agitated noises, stretching his wings now and then and looking a sight more ferocious than poor Arabella.

Pat eyed me sardonically from her garden.

"You'll need something bigger than *that* to put Charlemagne in his place!"

I felt as silly as Arabella should have done.

"Mrs Robbins gave her to me. I'd not thought . . ."

There was a large sticking plaster on the side of her hand which I couldn't help noticing as she handed over the bundle of frightened fur Arabella had become.

"What happened?" I asked, pointing to her hand.

"The screwdriver slipped." She shrugged.

"If I can help —"

"No thanks. I can manage."

Her stubborn chin told me she wouldn't trust another man for anything.

"Pat — about last night. I didn't mean —"

She shrugged off my apology.

"Why apologise for the truth? Not only do I destroy my own romance but everyone else's, too. It seems to come naturally."

I wished I could say something helpful, but I didn't know what to say. A disappointment after a few dates is one thing. Her own experience quite another.

WITHIN a very short time I became more expert at climbing trees than I ever had as a boy. Any small alarm, real or imaginary, would send Arabella shooting to the top of the pear tree without the nerve or know-how to come down again.

Once, she leapt onto the ladder Pat had left propped against the wall and was in the guttering crying with terror before I could try to stop her.

She was growing up fast, though. I began putting her outside before I went off to work, mainly for the sake of the furnishings, which were being shredded to bits, and my morning mail, which she liked to bat around the spacious hallway.

I hadn't caught more than a glimpse of Pat recently. Mrs Robbins informed, unasked, that she was having job interviews. The rest of the time, noises from next door told me she was working indoors.

One evening I came home and opened the back door just in time to hear a cry from the other side of the fence.

"Oh, *no*! Not my new garden chairs!"

Arabella came flying over the fence, all eyes and piteous complaint at being shouted at.

"Quiet, you cry baby!" I admonished, and went to look over the fence.

Pat looked startlingly elegant in a vivid blue suit and a pale custard shirt which matched her hair.

"She's clawed my covers to *bits*!"

Even from where I stood I could see threads dangling. Arabella had spent a busy day.

"I'm so sorry. I'll pay for new ones."

She gave me a long sigh. "I shouldn't have left them outside while I wasn't here. Forget it. Just say we're quits."

She made a throwaway gesture as if to say truce had been declared and disappeared indoors.

As I gazed after her, bemused by the lack of fireworks, I became aware that there was something different about her porch.

Then I realised — the pigeon roost had been removed. Had something happened to him? Maybe that was the reason she was subdued.

I'd buy her the chair covers, anyway, I decided. She'd had enough problems.

When I asked Mrs Robbins where I could buy them she shook her head. "I can run them up for next to nothing, Harry. It's indirectly my fault for letting Arabella loose on the two of you, anyway. I can't finish them in time for Saturday, though, and I expect she got them for extra seating. She's borrowing my pouffe and a couple of kitchen chairs for the barbecue. You're going, aren't you?"

Going? Going where?

"I haven't been invited," I said, bemused.

"Oh, but I'm sure you will be," Mrs Robbins assured me comfortably. "The whole of the street has been invited to the barbecue. And Pat's friends, of course."

Everybody but me, by the look of it, I thought glumly as I let myself back indoors.

Arabella abandoned the soggy piece of paper she'd been playing mouse with in the hall, and embraced my ankles.

I simply couldn't face yet more mail from the bank manager, so I didn't bother hunting the hall for my letters but fed Arabella instead.

"It's nice to be loved," I told her wryly.

On Saturday morning there were noises from next door. A deep masculine voice was making jokes as its owner assembled the barbecue. I heard Pat's laughter for the first time, warm and infectious.

"Jim, you're marvellous. Thanks for the help, what would I do without you?"

"Anything for you, Patsy, my love. Only hope the weather holds. They said thunderstorms later. Never mind — it'll be cosy indoors."

I felt so left out and lonely I couldn't even feel guilty about eavesdropping.

About nine o'clock I opened my back door to scrape burned toast on to the lawn. I couldn't seem to concentrate on anything.

The night was close and humid and there was not a star to be seen, but the glow of the barbecue spread above the fence and illuminated the knotholes. I quelled a desire to peep through.

"Come on, Arabella," I said. "Special treat — sardines."

She wasn't there.

"Oh! A cat's got my chicken leg!" shrieked a voice.

I scooted down the garden and through Pat's back gate.

I meant to grab Arabella and vanish, but before I could locate her the sky was split by a vivid sheet of lightning.

Two terrified green eyes lit up like lamps in the following darkness just to my right, and her yowl as she took off up the pear tree was drowned by thunder.

"No!" I yelled, starting after her. Then my toe caught in a root and I pitched forward, banging my shins painfully on the edge of the patio.

The guest were rushing indoors with chairs and cushions and food as the rain came slashing down.

In seconds, it seemed, I was alone with the sound of Arabella's wails from the top of the pear tree. The rain was like a curtain. I tried to stand up, but subsided again with a groan as a sharp pain suddenly shot up my legs.

"Harry?" Sandals slapped across the patio, a pair of wet feet appeared under my nose and long wet hair clung to my face like seaweed as Pat bent over me. She ran a gentle exploratory hand over my head.

"What have you done? Harry? Oh, help somebody! Help!"

Happily, she didn't stand a chance of being heard.

"Don't send for the fire brigade," I said carefully. "We're wet enough already."

She snatched her hand away, which I regretted. Not only had I outlived my penchant for petite brunettes, like Gillian, but I'd fallen in love with a hostile Amazon who only cared for a bird and somebody called Jim.

"Pat — what happened to Charlemagne?" I asked.

"Uncle took him back. He was pining for his friends. And stopping me from making one."

"And what about Jim?"

"*Jim*? What about him? He's my cousin — only more like a brother. We grew up together."

"For goodness' sake get up!"

"I like it here." I sighed, resting my head against her soggy, cotton-clad knees. "You mean — you wanted to be friends with me?"

"Harry — *will* you get up!"

"I could lie here for ever feeling your knees blush."

"Idiot!" She laughed softly. "You didn't even answer my note! I thought you didn't want to come to my party —"

"What note?" I asked. Then with a flash of insight I remembered Arabella's football with the letters the other day. "Oh, no," I wailed. "I have the feeling Arabella got there first. And talking of Arabella . . ."

Then before I could make a second attempt to struggle to my feet, a streak of fur leapt at me and burrowed inside my shirt.

"She's come down by herself! She must have overcome her fear of heights, Harry." Pat sighed. "Wish I had. I hate ladders. Have to whistle for courage."

I made a mental note of that. It was the beginning of all I wanted to discover about this girl. ∎

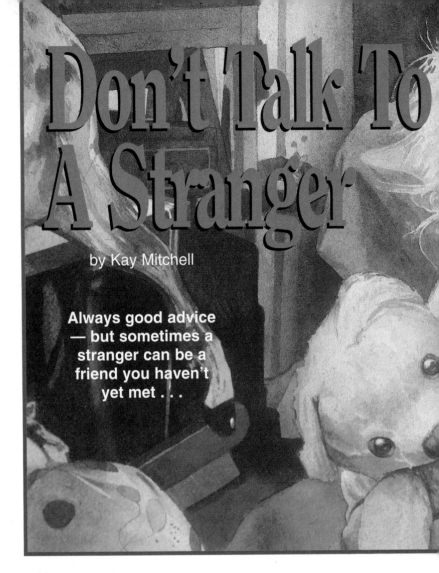

Don't Talk To A Stranger

by Kay Mitchell

Always good advice — but sometimes a stranger can be a friend you haven't yet met . . .

SHE was a thin waif of a child, sitting alone and silent on the park bench by the pond, her eyes fixed on the half-dozen ducks swimming around near the bank. From my vantage point on the path at the top of the grassy rise behind her I couldn't see the whole of her face; only her profile.

But she stirred in me a half-forgotten memory . . .

Of course! She reminded me of the doll.

My beloved Raggedy Ann, who'd gone to bed with me, cried with me, had measles with me. A cloth doll with spindly arms and legs, and straggly wool hair that fell straight and flat on both sides of her face.

Not a terribly pretty doll — but I wanted to keep on walking, because the solitary figure on the bench had nothing to do with me. Just as the rest of the world had nothing to do with me.

But something in the droop of the girl's shoulders held me there, watching her. She half turned her head as if she had felt my eyes on her. Then she went back to watching the ducks.

There were other people in the park. A group of boys over by the swings, people walking dogs, two or three couples holding hands. But the child — she could have been no more than ten — seemed to be on her own.

I sighed and turned away. It was then I saw that someone else was watching her, too. A man in a short, grubby jacket, standing quite still near a clump of tall rhododendrons.

Uneasy, I hesitated again. The sandwiches I hadn't eaten at lunch-time were still in my bag. If I took them home I would only throw them away. Better by far to feed them to the ducks.

When I sat down, the child seemed to shrink into herself. She didn't look at me, but neither did she run way.

I opened up the foil packet and laid it on the seat between us. Then I took a sandwich and began to break it up. The ducks squabbled and quacked, paddling and back-paddling furiously in their efforts to gobble the most bread.

Out of the corner of my eye, I saw the child's thin shoulders straighten a little.

"Would you like to throw some?"

The words were out before I'd even thought what to say and I felt mildly surprised. But she shook her head.

"I'd be grateful if you did really," I said, "because I don't have very much time."

This time her head turned and she looked directly at me. Her eyes were almost coal dark, but they didn't look like a child's eyes. They were old and wary. Still she said nothing. So I pushed the sandwiches closer to her and turned my attention back to the ducks.

When she took a sandwich her movement was quick, as if she expected the packet to be snatched away. She broke the bread carelessly and threw it clumsily so that some of it fell short of the water.

"I think they like it," I said. "Have you noticed the fat one in the middle? He's terribly greedy. He seems to gobble up twice as much bread as the others."

Again she looked at me and I held my breath. Suddenly, and without reason, it seemed terribly important to me to break through her silence, and I willed her to speak.

"Mrs Brady says I'm not to talk to strangers."

The words, when they came, put me firmly in my place.

"Mrs Brady, whoever she is, is quite right," I agreed.

Her hand edged towards the remaining sandwich and hesitated.

"It's all right," I said. "You break it up for them."

"Half each." She broke it scrupulously into two halves.

When the last piece had been thrown she stood up. "I've got to go now."

"Can I walk with you?" I asked. She said neither yes nor no, but instead turned suspicious eyes on me.

"I got to hurry 'cos I'm late."

And before I could say anything else she was running down the path in her too-long coat.

I walked behind her, annoyed that I, who didn't want to be involved with anyone ever again, should feel an urge to make sure a strange child got safely out of the park.

The next morning, after I had made my lunch sandwiches, there were two crusts of bread left in the packet. I took them with me almost without thinking.

When I left the office at five o'clock there was a sharp, chill breeze blowing and it seemed foolish to suppose the child might be in the park. But I turned up the collar of my coat and took the path that led past the duck pond.

She was there again, sitting on the bench, her thin shoulders hunched even more against the cold.

This time there were no ducks swimming on the edge of the pond; obviously they had more sense than either of us.

I SAT at the end of the seat, leaving a space between us. "Hi." She turned her head and the dark coals were empty of expression. "They've gone," she said, and sounded desolate. "Who?" I asked. "The ducks have gone. I thought they'd be here, but they've gone, too."

And I knew that whatever else I did that day, I had to find those ducks, wherever they were hiding, and prove to her that they hadn't left.

"I brought some bread for them," I showed her the crusts. "I expect they've found a sheltered spot somewhere, out of the wind. If you like we could have a look for them."

She shook her head and stared at the water.

"I'm absolutely sure they haven't gone away," I said. "And it seems a shame to take the bread home.

"Who knows, perhaps they're sitting somewhere quacking away to each other and complaining that all the people have gone away . . ."

She looked at me again, and I knew that this time she was trying to weigh me up; deciding by some strange logic of her own if I were to be trusted.

Then she got up and stood stiffly, facing me. "All right."

The words were neither eager, nor yet unwilling; as if in some way she was covering herself against the possibility of disappointment.

And I wondered what had happened to this hurt little girl, to make her so wary.

PERHAPS that was why I had allowed her through my own defences: because I had sensed a fellow sufferer. "There's a wooden shelter under the willow at the far end of the pond," I suggested. "In winter the ducks go there to roost when the weather is bad. Perhaps they're there, now."

The child's face brightened and for the first time really looked child-like. "I didn't know that," she said, eyes shining.

"You haven't walked around the pond?" I asked her.

She started to push her feet along the path as if she were skating, scattering small pieces of gravel. "Mrs Brady said I was to keep to the path if I walked through the park."

Sensible Mrs Brady again. But why not *Mum?* Mrs Brady might be her teacher; even so . . .

"Don't any grown-ups come to the park with you?" I asked.

"Nope."

"Never?"

"Nope. Mrs Brady says 'sometime', but she hasn't been yet. I think she'd like to come but she's always so busy and sort of flustered. I suppose because she's got six of us kids to look after."

"And does Mrs Brady live near here?"

"Down Neville Street." She stopped in the middle of the path and glowered at me. "What d'you want to know for? Are you a social worker?"

"No." I shook my head. "I work in an office." I looked across the park. "Look, do you see that very tall building over there? That's where I work, on the third floor from the top."

She looked to where my finger pointed and back to my face, her eyes full of doubt.

"When we walk around the next clump of rhododendrons," I said, forcing cheerfulness into my voice, "we'll be able to see the duck shelter."

Would she walk with me?

I strode forward and after a minute heard her feet scuffling behind me.

"Thought you might be another one."

I turned my head. "Another social worker, you mean?"

"Yeah."

"Well, I'm not." We rounded the bushes and could see the wooden shelter, built on stilts at the edge of the lake. Two of the missing ducks were swimming nearby.

"Ducks!" Surprise, relief, and admiration vied in her voice.

"Here." I handed her the crusts of bread. "If you feed these two, I expect the others will soon appear."

This time there was no hesitation; she took the bread and ran ahead of me. When I caught up she was watching the flurries of water as the other ducks took to the lake.

Questions that I wanted to ask her tumbled across my mind. But like all questions, there had to be a right time, and I didn't think that time was now.

P HILIP would have known of course. He was always so sensitive about other people's feelings. Pain rushed through my mind as it always did when I thought of Philip. After the funeral, well-meaning friends had said things would get better, that I'd get over his death. Perhaps in some ways I had.

But then would come a time when I needed his strength, his gentle understanding, and a great aching void would open up inside me. As it did now.

Having thrown the last of the bread, the child suddenly turned and saw my face. Her eyes opened wide and startled, and then, suddenly, filled with understanding.

She didn't say anything, but she slipped her hand into mine and held it silently as I took deep gulps of air.

"I'm sorry I thought you was a social worker," she said, and I squeezed her hand gently as we began to walk back the way we had come.

"Mrs Brady says social workers are a necessary evil. I just think they're a blooming nuisance. What do you think?"

Surprisingly I felt the pain recede.

"I'm not sure," I told her cautiously. "I only know one, and I went to school with her, so that makes it different."

"I've had six social workers." I caught a hint of pride in her voice.

"And Mrs Brady?" I asked softly. "Who is she?"

"She's a foster-mum. I've had three of them, too."

"That's quite a lot," I said.

"And I been in two Homes."

"And you didn't like it anywhere?"

"I liked me mum, but she went away. And I liked me first foster-mum, but when she had a baby she sent me away. I like Mrs Brady, I suppose. But she's always so busy. She never has time to spare just to listen. And that house is so crowded. So I come here. It's private — my own private place."

"Well," I said, "I'd like to share your private place, if you wouldn't mind. My name is Linda, Linda Barr. Will you tell me your name?"

"Lucy Penny." We had reached the park gates and she let go of my hand. "I expect I'll be in the park tomorrow."

"I expect I will too," I agreed.

"See you then," she said, and ran off down the pavement out of sight.

Philip would have said there had to be a purpose to my meeting Lucy. But Philip thought there was a purpose to everything.

I often wished that I felt the same. And yet . . .

The more I thought about Lucy, the more the feeling grew on me that perhaps, just perhaps, Lucy needed the kind of friendship that I could give her. I let myself into the small flat that I had bought when Philip died, and changed out of my office clothes.

When I'd moved in everything was new. No memories. The photographs that had been dotted around the house were put away into drawers, so that I shouldn't see them.

Only that way, I told myself, would I ever stop missing him.

But it didn't work. A year later I missed him as much as ever.

Meeting Lucy in the park after work became a ritual, and one that I looked forward to. She talked to me about school, about things that Mrs Brady said, and about her mother . . .

"She got fed up of looking after me," she said philosophically. "That's why she went away. I expect Mrs Brady will get fed up eventually, too."

"But you like Mrs Brady, don't you?"

"That doesn't make no difference, does it? I liked me mum, too."

Spring became summer. Lucy shed her coat and woolly hat. The ducks seemed to anticipate our coming, gathering each day on the bank to wait, and leaping back into the water at the first sight of bread. Sometimes Lucy, too, brought crusts.

"Mrs Brady says she don't mind as long as I don't fall in," she said.

For an adult and child we covered many subjects. I even told her about the flat and how empty it felt.

I wasn't even surprised when she understood.

She asked exactly where it was, so she could picture me in it, she said. I told her, so touched I could barely speak.

Amazingly, or at least it seemed that way to me, the more I thought about Lucy, the more my own pain receded. Gradually I found that I could think about the good things that Philip and I had shared.

Then, one Wednesday, I went to work feeling unwell, with an upset stomach and a headache.

About one o'clock in the afternoon the pain in my stomach settled into a raging torment and I found myself rushed to hospital.

When I learned that I had appendicitis all I could think about was that Lucy would be waiting for me.

But it was a week before I thought about her again, as a ruptured appendix led to peritonitis.

When I finally surfaced from a mixture of drugs and pain, to find my mother sitting by the bed, Lucy was the first thought in my mind.

"Please, Mum," I asked her. "Go to the park at five o'clock and look for her."

Lucy wasn't there, of course. Not that day, nor the next.

I suppose, I thought miserably, she would think *I* had got tired of her, too.

WHEN I got out of hospital I spent a week at my mother's home, convalescing, and then went back to my flat. My mother had popped round there a few times while I was ill, to dust and pick up the mail from behind the door.

"Would you like me to bring your post in for you?" she had asked, just before I came out of hospital. And I told her no; there would be nothing that couldn't wait.

But there had been.

A grubby, bent envelope with my name scrawled in childish writing.

The message inside was simple and to the point.

I thought you were my friend. Nothing else.

I looked at the note and the tears that ran from my eyes were for Lucy, not for me.

For three days I haunted the park, but there was no Lucy. Eventually, I gathered up my courage and went to Neville Street to find Mrs Brady.

"Lucy's not here," the harassed-looking woman told me when she answered the door. With one hand she pushed her hair away from her eyes, the other held a beaming toddler. From indoors, came the sound of childish bickering.

"I suppose you're the one she used to meet in the park. Well when you stopped coming, Lucy ran away." She sighed. "Three times. The first twice they brought her back, but the third time the social worker took her away.

"I don't even know where she is now." Her eyes filled with tears and she made to close the door, obviously blaming me. I stopped the door with my hand.

"Please," I begged. "I've been in hospital. I must find her."

Her eyes searched mine and what she saw there must have satisfied her, because her face softened.

"You'd better come in a minute," she said.

HER sitting-room was a clutter of odds and ends, warm and homely. Toys were scattered over the rug and two five-year-olds were squabbling over a doll's house. Mrs Brady smiled apologetically at me.

"As you can see, I have enough on my plate. I took Lucy because she was a problem — no-one else would have her. I suppose it was a mistake because I didn't have enough time to devote to her.

"Lucy's been let down rather a lot in her short life," she finished.

"I know," I said unhappily.

"Her mother left her to the council, and there's no knowing who her father is." She scribbled on a pad that lay beside the telephone and tore off the top sheet.

"John Redmond is her social worker, this is his telephone number. You'll find him at the office next to the town hall. I hope they'll let you see her."

"Thank you." I put the paper in my handbag and walked back gratefully to the outside door.

"If you do see her," Mrs Brady said, "I'd like to know how she is. And give her my love."

"I'll come and tell you," I promised.

THE next morning I went to see Lucy's social worker, a dark-haired, bearded man in his late 20s. "I wanted to ask about Lucy Penny," I began, and told him what had happened. He listened without interrupting.

"Lucy is back in a children's home," he told me eventually. "She's being reassessed. That's not as bad as it sounds. It means she will be seen by a child psychologist again, so that we can know the best thing to do for her."

"Can I see her?" The request was blunt.

"How long were you and your husband married?" he asked without answering.

"A year. Why? I don't see that that has anything to do with my seeing Lucy."

"I need to know your motives. People do things for funny reasons

119

sometimes. I have to look at Lucy's needs, not yours, I'm afraid."

I stared at him. "You think I'm making Lucy a substitute for Philip. Well, I'm not. It's Lucy I'm thinking of. I don't want her to think I let her down, too."

"That's for now," he said, "but what about the future? Can you offer Lucy a long-term commitment? Because if not it would be better to leave things as they are."

I felt angry with him. "Lucy has to know why I didn't come."

He nodded. "I agree. But I can tell her that. What I'm asking is — for how long would you be prepared to be a friend to Lucy?"

"As long as she needs me."

"And not as long as you need her?"

This man certainly had a way with words, they were like barbs and couldn't be easily dismissed.

I thought about Lucy and my own life. Yes, she had helped to lessen my grief, I couldn't deny that. But that wasn't why I wanted to find her again. Was it?

I stared down at my hands, thinking. Inside my head I seemed to hear Philip's voice, warm, reassuring. *There is nothing without a purpose.*

"As long as *she* needs *me*," I said firmly, looking directly into John Redmond's eyes.

He nodded. "I hoped you would say that." He looked at his watch.

"I'll find someone to take over here. Then I'll drive you to the children's home. It's not far."

"Thank you."

He started to go out of the door and hesitated. "There is one thing you must be prepared for," he said quietly.

"Lucy may not want to see you."

THE Home was 15 miles away, in a neighbouring town. A tall old house with gardens on three sides. John took me into a comfortable waiting-room, with easy chairs, and went to find Lucy. When the door opened and he came in alone, my heart sank.

Lucy didn't want to see me. Then I caught a glimpse of pink behind him.

"Someone here to see you," he said, and Lucy came into the room.

She stood silently, and her eyes were wary again; she looked thinner than ever. I held out my arms.

"Oh, Lucy," I said. "I've missed you so much."

She took a half-step forward and stopped. "I looked for you and you weren't there," she accused.

"I couldn't be," I pleaded. "I was in the hospital. I was ill."

She looked from me to John. He nodded.

"I looked for you, too," I told her. "When I came home. I went to the park. When you weren't there I went to see Mrs Brady."

"And Mrs Brady sent her to see me," John added.

"I really have missed you," I said again. This time she threw herself into my arms and her bones felt thin and brittle as I held her.

I stayed for a half-hour and then John had to leave.

"Will you come for tea tomorrow?" Lucy asked before I left. "I can have visitors. You get jam and bread and cake," she added as a bribe.

"I'll come," I said. "I promise."

"I'd like to foster Lucy," I said as John drove me home. "I thought that might be on your mind. It wouldn't be roses all the way, you know. I don't doubt that Lucy will give problems as she grows up."

"We could work them out."

"Think about it for a few days. If you're still keen I'll come and see you."

"And then?"

"And then," he said, "if I'm satisfied it would be best for Lucy, I'll call a case conference and suggest that as the best course of action."

THAT was a year ago, and since then Lucy and I have learned to live together happily in spite of a few bumps along the way. Today she is 11, and a pink and white birthday cake that she helped me to make is sitting on the table ready for tea.

On the shelf, and on the bookcase, are photographs of Philip and me together.

Most of the pain has gone, and I have even managed to forgive the drunken driver who caused his death; as I know Philip would want me to do.

"It's lucky you got appendicitis," John said to me on his last visit.

"Because if she hadn't I would still be at Mrs Brady's, you mean?" Lucy asked.

"That's right!" He laughed and rested his hand on my shoulder. It felt warm and reassuring. "And you and I would never have met," he whispered to me. Then, for Lucy's benefit, added, "Which just goes to show that everything happens for a purpose."

Philip would approve of John. I'm sure of it. ■

More Than Words Can Say...

**There are many ways of describing this story.
We would simply say — it's a love story in the deepest
sense of the word . . .**

by Mary Pache

N one hour my daughter will be here. I can be so precise because June is telephoning from the café where she breaks her journey, and it is one hour's drive away. "Have you brought Kerry with you?" I dare to ask, after the brisk enquiries and replies. The pips bleat monotonously and are followed by the relentless click.

A sudden sigh makes my shoulders tremble, and tells me that I've been holding my breath. It's so long since Kerry came. So long.

When she arrives, June will give me the usual hug and kiss, then stand back with her hands on my shoulders to scrutinise my face.

I will see a reflection of my own anxiety draw lines between her eyes. She will look upwards, questioningly.

"And how is she?" my daughter will say.

"She" is Fay, my wife and June's mother, who has heard our telephone conversation and has rushed upstairs to the bedroom.

She is dragging all the lighter pieces of furniture to form a barricade in front of the door, now.

The approach of strangers frightens her, and for the first hour of her visit June is seen as a stranger.

"About the same," I will answer.

"It's too much for you, Dad," she will say, in a warning voice. And her meaning will lie heavily between us.

I will search for words to explain once more how it is with Fay and me. That being old makes no difference. That her sickness makes no difference.

But your feet are planted so firmly in the practical world, June. Will you ever glimpse the charm of Fay's fairy world?

"I don't suppose you've had a proper meal since I was here last," she will continue, and I will nod in agreement.

Fay never was a housewife, and now she obstructs my efforts to clean and cook. I would be angry, except that when her eyes shine with the mischief of her second childhood it takes me back to her first; to hers and mine, when she was the quicksilver of the school playground.

"Your name can't be Edna," I'd once cried out in disbelief. Then, firmly, "I shall always call you Fay."

I smile as I remember.

June will then survey the disorder of the kitchen and bite her lip, and the worry lines will deepen.

I will think, yet again, that she had to grow up too soon. She shouldered the responsibilities of running the home when she was only a schoolgirl, and Fay was darting from one enthusiasm to another as the fancy took her.

June will prepare the food she has brought with her. Last time it was home-made steak pie, with potatoes and greens, and a syrup pudding. She will put aside a third plate and cover it.

AS we eat we will talk about Brian, June's husband, and her two teenage sons. I will ask about Kerry, their "afterthought", a gift from Fay's fairyland, with her wisp of a figure and the streaming, tawny-orange hair. In the spaces between our talk, we will listen to the sounds of the barricade being removed — stealthily, piece by piece. Then Fay's light footfalls will sound on the stairs.

I will feel a spurt of joy as she comes into the room, and June will look from one of us to the other. She will frown slightly, as if she is trying to solve a riddle.

Did you know you were the odd one out right from the beginning, June? We'd lived for each other, Fay and I, for half a lifetime. You came late when, like innocents, we'd forgotten about the possibility.

You have Brian, but I sense that you've never felt our sort of magic . . .

Fay will sit down and uncover her plate. She will eat and join in the conversation. We will be like an ordinary family, a daughter visiting her parents.

It will be as if Fay's disturbing episodes have never happened.

I can predict so exactly because these weekends, one in four, have followed the same pattern ever since June found out that Fay is . . . not herself.

There is one difference today. This is the third weekend, not the fourth, and June has broken the pattern because it is my birthday.

I can hear the car now, and the decisive grind of the handbrake. Have I been here, sitting by the phone, for a whole hour, thinking my own thoughts? I reach for a coat.

"Hello, there!" I call as I walk out into the mild, dry January day to meet them.

June is holding the car door open, and a slip of an elfin creature dances out.

"Kerry!" I shout, and catch her as she runs into my arms. She looks more like Fay than ever.

I stroke her hair and its colour paints a picture in my mind's eye — of Fay, with hers floating free of its week-day plait, as she leapt in and out of a skipping rope.

"Happy birthday, Grandad!" Kerry bubbles, and I sit on the garden seat and unwrap the tie she has chosen for me herself.

SHE climbs astride my knee and fixes it round my neck in her fumbling, five-year-old fashion. "I've left the boys behind with Brian," June tells me. "They all send their love but they've an important football match to win. School trophy."

I look away, disappointed yet knowing they couldn't let their team-mates down, and knowing too, that their granny's funny ways embarrass them. But Kerry is here, and June so enjoys my delight in her, she forgets to ask the usual questions.

Kerry runs through to the back garden and I follow, marvelling at the stream of tawny orange.

I washed Fay's hair yesterday. I dried and brushed it, lingering over the task of love until it was a shining river of silver.

Kerry greets an old pile of dry leaves with a squeal, and leaps into it. Now she is laughing through the tangle and aiming handfuls at me. I return them, and soon the leaves are scattered.

I bring the big coloured ball from the shed. I've been keeping it so long, hoping she would come. We throw and catch, keeping warm and she shows me how long she can keep it bouncing.

June calls us in to eat. It's toad-in-the-hole today, with chips and cauliflower with the covered plate beside us.

A growing sense of something missing makes me pause.

I realise that there have been no sounds of the barricade being removed.

June stops with a forkful of food halfway to her mouth. She puts it down suddenly, excuses herself, and goes upstairs.

I follow slowly, so slowly that June meets me on her way down. Her eyes are diamond bright, and the lines have jumped back between them.

I don't need to be told that the barricade has gone, and so has Fay.

"You stay with Kerry, Dad. I'll go and ask the neighbours."

Something is pounding unevenly in my chest.

Please, I beg silently. Not the neighbours this time. Not now that their anger has faded to careful politeness after Fay, with her strange new obsession with money, made door to door calls selling scraps of clothing at three o'clock one morning.

"She ought to be in a home!" was the indignant exclamation I heard again and again.

Fay is in a home. With me, where she belongs.

June returns, shaking her head.

I pray that this is one of Fay's normal days. Perhaps she is taking our library books back, or the washing to the launderette . . . I am afraid to check on these things, in case I am proved wrong.

I hear June spin the telephone dial three times. I breathe in so sharply that it hurts. The police found her on a train to Penzance, once.

I try not to remember that they found her crossing the motorway last time, wanting to pick the wild flowers on the central reservation.

I try not to remember, but I know that I have because my legs are shaky and I sit down suddenly.

Kerry kneels in front of me and looks gravely into my face. Are those my tears falling on her little hands?

June appears in the doorway.

"It's too much for you, Dad." A statement this, with the hint of a threat. "They would look after her in a nursing home."

"I look after her."

THERE is urgent rapping at the front door. June goes to open it, and Fay walks in grandly, carrying a square white box with both hands. She sweeps the dinner plates aside and places it in the centre of the table, then releases the ribbon with a dramatic gesture.

Kerry skips about, her excitement bursting out in little trills.

"It's Grandad's birthday cake!"

June and I look at each other and her face lifts in a smile. Now we know the reason for the hoarding of money.

Kerry is puzzled.

"Grandad's ancient," she says. "We must have lots of candles. Why are you only putting one on his cake?"

"One candle, one love," someone says softly. But it isn't Fay's voice, it's June's.

Our eyes meet and my burden suddenly loses it weight. Relief breaks over me like a healing wave. At last I can admit to myself that the day will come, perhaps soon, when the bonds of my love must be loosened. But at least then I'll know that June understands why every moment with her mother is precious.

In a swift change of mood, Fay has whisked Kerry away to the end of the garden, and they are playing together on the grass.

June tucks her arm in mine.

And together we walk down the path to the fairy world.■

Those Lonely Nights

by Sarah Burkhill

He had the most uncanny feeling that the same circumstances which had drawn them together were about to tear them apart.

DEBBIE is playing in the back garden with Patch, as she usually does after tea if the weather is fine. Three months ago, when I first came up from Birmingham, I used to watch her sometimes from the kitchen window as I cooked my meal. An attractive child with lovely black hair, like a miniature version of the woman I saw occasionally hanging out washing or taking rubbish to the communal bins at the back.

We had never spoken. The furnished flat was just a base for me while I supervised the computerisation of our northern offices, and getting to know the neighbours seemed a bit pointless.

Sometimes, though, I had wondered about the woman.

There didn't seem to be any man on the scene. Was she a single parent? A divorcée, perhaps, or a widow?

She always seemed harassed, which was a pity, for if the tense, anxious face had relaxed into a smile she would have been almost beautiful.

That first day we met, however, out by the front pathway, her expression was weary and impatient.

"Oh, for goodness' sake, Debbie, stop howling," she was saying. "There's nothing we can do about it now."

I smiled and nodded to her, then turned to the little girl.

She was breaking her heart, tears streaming down her face.

"Hey, what's up, chicken?" I asked.

"Jamie!" She gulped. "Jamie's got lost!"

Her mother shook her head in exasperation.

"Her doll," she explained. "The playgroup had them all out at the park this morning, and she must have left it there.

"We went back and looked, but there was no sign of it."

"He'll have *drowned!*" Debbie said dramatically. "We were at the pond, catching minnows. He'll have fallen in the water and got *drowned!*"

SHE started wailing again, and I crouched down beside her, straining my neck to avoid Patch licking my face. "Jamie?" I remembered the doll that always accompanied her on her after-tea forays in the garden. "Little fellow about so-high, in blue dungarees and a red shirt?"

She nodded.

"Oh, he didn't get drowned," I assured her solemnly. "I met him coming up the street not half an hour ago.

"He's gone adventuring."

The tears stopped suddenly, as if someone had turned a tap off, and she looked wonderingly at me.

"Where to?"

I spread my hands.

"Who knows? You don't always have a plan in mind when you go off to seek your fortune.

"But he'll be all right, I promise. He asked me to tell you goodbye, and that he'd be in touch soon."

She was staring thoughtfully at me.

"But — but why did he go away?" She frowned. "Why did he want to go away from me ad — adventuring?"

"Because he's a boy doll," I said firmly. "And boy dolls like to go off and see the world.

"Isn't that right?" I looked to her mother for confirmation, hoping she wasn't a women's libber and against such blatant sexism. I was relieved to see her smiling.

128

"But you mustn't worry. You'll probably hear from him very soon.

"In fact," I added, "I wouldn't be a bit surprised if you got a postcard next week."

"Very clever," the woman said archly as Debbie ran on after the dog, her eyes wide with this new prospect to look forward to.

"But not original," I confessed, grinning. "The story is attributed to Franz Kafka, who got a flash of inspiration in similar circumstances.

"I read it in a magazine in a dentist's waiting-room."

"Well, original or not, it certainly stopped the waterworks. Thanks. She nearly had *me* at screaming point, too!"

We walked up the path together and caught up with Debbie at the first door.

"Are you settling in all right? When I saw the top flat was occupied again, I did mean to pop up and ask if there was anything I could do, but — well, it's been a hectic couple of weeks," she finished apologetically.

"There wasn't much settling to do," I replied. "I'm more or less living out of a suitcase — I'll only be here for a few months."

I explained about the job, then added, "I'm Bruce Chalmers, by the way."

"Fay Neilson." She smiled again as she turned the key in the door and shepherded child and dog inside.

"Thanks again. And if there's anything you need, give us a shout, will you?"

I HAD no more contact with either of them until Saturday of the next week when, on my return from the supermarket, I found Debbie waiting for me. "He *wrote!*" she announced, her eyes shining. She waved the postcard at me.

"Look! It says . . . what does it say, Mummy?" she called back through the open door.

I took the card from her and read aloud, "It says, 'Dear Debbie, I'm in London now and having a great time. Sorry I couldn't tell you I was going away, but I don't like goodbyes. Will write again soon. Love, Jamie.'"

I gave it back to her. "See? I told you he'd write, didn't I?"

Fay Neilson appeared at the door, mouthing a thank you.

"Hi! How's it going?" she said. "D'you want a coffee? I've just put the kettle on."

"Well — if —"

"Come in and I'll show you my other dolls," Debbie insisted, dragging me by the cuff. "I've got Rachel, and Sylvia, and . . ."

By the time I'd been introduced to the family, Fay had reappeared with a tray.

"I bet they wish they could go adventuring, too," Debbie said. "But they can't, can they? 'Cause they're girl dollies, and girl dollies don't do that, do they?"

"Rôle stereotyping!" Fay twisted down the corners of her mouth. "You'd get dogs' abuse from the feminists, encouraging an attitude like that!"

Debbie saved me the trouble of replying by cutting in.

"Maybe my daddy will meet Jamie," she said. "My daddy stays near London, doesn't he?"

"Uh-huh. And you'll be staying there too, soon."

Fay passed a plate of biscuits.

"Murray's working in the South just now," she told me. "It's just a six-month contract initially, but he's pretty hopeful they'll keep him on afterwards, then we'll all move down."

I took a Digestive. "It must be difficult for you both. The separation, I mean."

She shrugged.

"Not much option, is there? He'd been unemployed for almost nine months, and there's very little in the way of prospects for him round here.

"We had to sell our house over at Greenacre, and rent this place."

She looked sad for a moment then shrugged again.

"Still, things seem to be working out better now.

"And it's worse for Murray than for me, of course. It can't be much fun for him, all on his own in a dingy little bedsit, so far away from anyone he knows."

"It *isn't* much fun," I said with feeling. "Although I've probably done a bit better accommodation-wise!"

"Of course." She took my cup. "You're in the same boat, aren't you?

"How long did you say you were going to be here?"

We talked for a while about my work, and my home in Birmingham, then I thanked her for the coffee and got up to go.

"It was nice of you to send her the postcard," Fay said at the door. "She really believes it came from London and she's over the moon about it, really she is."

She hesitated a moment, then went on. "Look — would you like to come down and have some supper with us this evening?

"I was just thinking — I'd be glad if Murray had some friendly neighbours to take him under their wing occasionally.

"It'll only be something simple, but if you'd like . . ."

I held up my supermarket carrier, with its rapidly-thawing frozen dinner for one.

"Anything at all would be better than this," I declared. "I'd love to, thanks."

PATCH is barking excitedly as he chases his ball, and Debbie, catching sight of me, waves up at the window. I smile and return the wave, then let the net curtain drop back into place. It was a nice evening, that Saturday three months ago, and we repeated it the following week.

Was it stupid of us? In retrospect, yes. A young married woman entertaining a strange man while her husband was working away. Even amongst the most pure-minded of people it would have been enough to set tongues wagging.

But at the time there seemed no harm in it.

To Fay it was just a friendly gesture to someone in circumstances similar to her husband's.

And to me — well, it was a change, I suppose. The chance of a good home-cooked meal and some pleasant company after a hard week.

Probably Debbie's presence lent an air of respectability as well, though on the second evening I sat on for a while after she'd gone to bed.

"Come on, help me finish off this wine," Fay said, picking up the bottle I'd brought.

"Murray phoned last night." She filled the two glasses. "He was supposed to be coming home for next weekend — this being the sort of halfway mark, so to speak.

"It's too expensive for him to travel back often, so we thought we'd split it. Three months there, then a visit home, then the other three months. Y'know?"

She sipped at the wine.

"But he's got the chance of some overtime for the next few weeks, and he doesn't want to pass it up.

"We'll need all the money we can get if we're to buy a house down there."

I looked up at the photograph on the mantelpiece. It showed Fay and Debbie and a nice-looking young man with a slow, easy smile, posed against the background of a red-brick house.

SHE followed my eyes, and gazed at the photograph as though it showed people she couldn't recognise. "It's just that — Oh, I get so fed up with it all! It's not even just the past while with him being down south. It — it seems like everything's been going wrong for ever, now."

She drank some more of the wine and returned the glass to the table with an unsteady hand.

"First it was Murray being made redundant, and us having to sell the house.

"Then watching him mope around all the time, getting more and more depressed and dispirited about everything.

"And even —" she rounded indignantly on me "— even when *I* got a part-time job, he made such a fuss about having to look after the house and Debbie for a bit that I'd to give it up!"

"I don't suppose it could have been very easy for him," I began slowly.

"I *know* it wasn't easy for him. But it wasn't easy for me either. And instead of being able to help each other through it, we just seemed to have rows all the time.

"And now —" she swallowed, "— now with him being away —"

Her eyes filled with tears that had been threatening for a long time, and she looked just like Debbie had on the first day we'd spoken.

"Hey," I went over and knelt beside her. "Come on, now. It'll be all right. It'll work out."

She drew her hand back from me and produced a paper tissue from her sleeve.

"I'm sorry, Bruce. I shouldn't be talking like this.

"I must sound — very disloyal."

"We've all got to talk to someone," I said. "Maybe it's easier with someone we don't really know too well."

She nodded and smiled half-heartedly.

"I know. That's the trouble, probably. There's been no-one I *could* talk to."

"With family and close friends you tend to bottle everything up and put a good face on it, because you don't want to worry them.

"And with Murray — well what can you say on the telephone? You can hardly off-load all the hassles of the week."

She bit her lip, then shrugged.

"Oh, pay no attention to me. It's just been a rotten few days. First Patch cut his paw and I'd to haul him along to the vet.

"Then my iron went on the blink and I'd to pay what seemed like a fortune for a new one.

"And *now* —" she gave an exaggerated sigh — "the flaming kitchen tap won't stop dripping!"

She laughed ruefully, and I bounced on to my feet again.

"Dogs and irons are beyond me," I admitted. "But fitting a washer should be easy enough, if that's all it needs.

"And talking of needs," I added firmly as we went through to the kitchen, "what *you* need, young lady, is taking out of yourself.

"How about coming for a drive with me tomorrow. You and Debbie can show me some of the sights?"

We went to Port Helen, and walked along a windswept promenade while Debbie insisted on taking off socks and shoes to paddle in the water with Patch.

"Oh, it's just so nice to get out of the city for a while!" Fay said. "It seems ages since we've been anywhere.

"Do you do a lot of travelling in your work, normally?"

"A fair bit. But usually just for a week or two at a time. The longer jobs — like this one — don't come up too often."

"It must get lonely for you, I suppose. Never being able to feel really settled, I mean," she added.

"Sometimes." I looked out over the vast expanse of sea. "But mostly it suits me well enough.

"I'm a bit of a workaholic." I grinned apologetically. "That's always been the most important thing to me."

We stopped to buy ice-cream at a van, the signal for Debbie to come racing back to us.

"It's been a lovely day," Fay said when we got home. "You were right, I did need to get out for a while."

It had been a lovely day for me, too. Silly, and happy, and — and fun. The kind of day I hadn't had in a long, long time.

I wondered if she told Murray about it and learned next month she had.

HE came home late on the Friday night, and stayed till Sunday. I'd been going to keep out of their way, but Fay came up and invited me to have a quick drink with them on the Saturday evening. He seemed a nice enough bloke — friendly and easy-going, though with that slightly disorientated manner of a person who lives and works in one place, but considers another place to be his home.

He talked to me about computers, and I talked to him about unemployment, and the weather, and the Middle East crisis — everything, except the fact that I was falling in love with his wife.

Couldn't he see it? Did it not occur to him that the situation was fraught with danger?

Maybe he was so taken up with the new life he was carving that he didn't think too much about what was happening back home.

Or maybe he was just naturally trusting, so secure in her love for him that he didn't realise the last year might have put such a strain on it.

Or perhaps — perhaps he was too frightened to upset their delicate balance by questioning what was, after all, no more than a casual friendship.

"Do you feel better about everything — now that you've seen him again?" I asked her during the next week.

"I suppose so. It was such a short time, though," she replied. "You feel — well — that you're just getting to know each other again, and then he's off.

"But one thing," she added, "it seems more or less certain that he'll get a permanent contract, so he's going to start looking round for a house soon."

"And then we'll be going away." Debbie announced as she came in from the garden. "Like Jamie did."

She took the latest postcard down from the sideboard. "Last week he was — where was he, again?"

"Aberdeen." Fay said. She gave me an exasperated smile and shook her head.

BRUCE, how are you going to get out of this?" she asked me two days later. Debbie had dragged me in to see the latest communications before she was packed off to bed. "I mean, you can't go on sending postcards for the rest of your life," she pointed out. "There must be only so many picture postcards showing fluffy animals and the Royal Family."

"Hmm. I know. It's getting more and more difficult," I told her seriously. "Well — this week he's in Ballymena and I'm not sure what kind of picture to buy.

"Next week I thought he could go on to Dublin — and from there he could stow away on a ship to Australia. That would put him incommunicado for some time, wouldn't it?"

She laughed, and I laughed with her.

It's funny how quickly the mood changes. One minute two people are laughing together, and then, as their eyes meet, the laughter fades.

"Anyway," I said, "she'll forget about it all soon.

"Sooner than I'll forget about you," I added.

I don't know which of us moved first. Did Fay lean towards me, or was it me who reached for her?

I don't know. It was like one of those slow-motion sequences in a film, with two people coming together as if finally reaching the place they belonged.

There was a damp smudge of mascara on her cheek when she pulled back from me, but she spoke quietly, as if in control.

"I love Murray," she said. "I know it hasn't been right with us lately, but I do love him. I do."

Her voice held a conviction that wasn't in her eyes. They were doubtful and confused, as if she had been startled in the middle of a dream, and couldn't quite separate it from reality.

"I know you do," I told her as she came into my arms again . . .

DEBBIE has gone indoors. It'll be her bedtime soon, so if I'm going down it will have to be now. I didn't see Fay last night. After my day at the Bridgedene office I went on for a meal with Charlie Harrison, the manager there.

It was past 11 when I returned, and a light still showed in the ground-floor flat. I went straight upstairs.

It's Debbie who opens the door to me now, as Fay comes out of the kitchen, drying her hands on a dish towel.

"Did you see me waving to you? From the garden?"

I can't meet Fay's eyes, but I know the confusion and uncertainty are still there.

"Uh-huh. Did you not see me wave back?"

Debbie nods, and I throw a mock punch at her. "Don't ask daft questions, then."

I swallowed, wishing I could take the easy way out, like Jamie had.

"I've come to say goodbye to you, chicken," I tell her. "I've got to go away, you see. Now. In fact I'm leaving tonight."

She looks suddenly crestfallen, but I can't glance up to see if Fay shares her expression.

134

I love him, she said. *I do love him.*

And of course she does. If I had never appeared she would have got through those bad months, and joined him, and everything would have been all right again, for the three of them.

But I did appear. And she was lonely and weary and sad after a difficult year.

It can happen so easily. I know that.

I, if anyone, should know that.

Perhaps if Erik Dixon had had the strength to walk away, Carolyn and I might still have been together.

She had been sad and lonely, too, tired of the all-too-frequent nights on her own, without even a child like Debbie for company.

Until she met Erik, that is. Until he was there for her when I couldn't be.

"But where are you going?" Debbie is asking.

"I'm going adventuring." I smile at her. "Like Jamie did. There's a whole big world out there, and we men have got to go and see it."

"And will you send me postcards, like Jamie?"

Fay has come forward, put a hand on the child's shoulder. I look up at her now, but whether it's pain or relief or sadness that fills her eyes, I can't tell.

"No, Debbie," I say. "After all, I won't know where to send them, will I?

"You'll be moving away soon, won't you? You'll be going to live with your daddy, in a lovely new house he's getting specially for you and Mum.

"Goodbye, pet. Take care, now."

I plant a kiss on her cheek, then reach out a hand to Fay.

"Good luck. I — I hope it all goes well for you."

★　★　★　★

And for you too, Bruce. Her steady, casual words still ring in my ears as I take the two suitcases out to the car.

She is drawing the curtains in the living-room, but she doesn't wave and neither do I.

Instead I just watch her for a brief moment, until the heavy tan material steals her from my view.

The pain will go, of course. Hers, and mine, too.

She has a new life to look forward to. This interlude will become just a part of a nightmarish year.

And I — well, as I said to Debbie, there's a whole big world out there.

Somewhere in it there will be someone I can care for without hurting — now that one special lady has taught me how to love again. ■

The Great

**Generosity isn't always what you do
for a person. Sometimes it's what you encourage
them to do for themselves . . .**

by Joyce Stranger

EVERYONE told Kane he could walk. The accident had damaged him, of course, but his legs had recovered. There was no reason at all why he shouldn't learn to run again; to play cricket again; to be strong again.

But Kane didn't believe them. His legs hurt if he tried to stand. He imagined himself falling again; and as he fell, he heard again the scream of brakes, felt the slam against his body, of the car that hadn't been able to stop. And he was terrified.

His parents tried encouragement and they tried anger. They tried teasing him, infuriating him and at last, after nine long months, they gave up.

Kane hated his legs. He hated lying still while others moved around him, and most of all he hated the driver of the car that had injured him so badly.

He was only 15 years old and had a lifetime ahead. But it would be a lifetime of lying still, of being unable to move except in a wheelchair. And people would always look at him with pitying faces. People who knew he wasn't part of the real world any more.

Kane lay day after day watching television. He read sometimes, but the books annoyed him — they were always about men who could race on two legs, could fly, could swim, could ride a bicycle or drive a car.

Men who could *live*.

He didn't believe people any more. He didn't believe the doctor who begged him to try to walk.

"It won't be easy, Kane, I know. But you *can* walk; I know you can."

I was easier just to lie still, and feel his anger grow. Kane snarled at his sister, snapped at his mother, trying to make them suffer as he suffered, all the time.

They bought him paints; but he didn't like painting. They bought him model kits, so that he could make motor cars, or aeroplanes, or jig-saws. He didn't want any of them.

The shadow of his misery blanketed the house, so that his sister preferred to be out with her friends, his mother's shoulders drooped and her mouth seemed thin and tight.

His father watched him with a brooding look, wishing that, somehow, he could get through to his son.

But there was nothing in the world Kane wanted to do — except be a normal boy again.

He didn't want to talk. He refused to take an interest in anything but himself. His friends visited at first but soon they, too, gave up.

Only his grandfather didn't give up.

He visited every month.

At first he brought gifts, small things to try to gain his grandson's interest.

Eventually, he brought nothing but himself. He sat by Kane's bed, remembering his own boyhood.

He talked of sunlight on the river and hours spent watching a heron fishing; he talked of the sea breaking on the beaches and the feel of sand under his bare feet; he talked of climbing the hill and standing on the summit to see the land, snowclad, spread out beneath him.

He talked of winter, he talked of spring; but most of all, he talked of hope.

He never knew whether Kane listened, but he went on, all the same.

Then, one day, he brought another gift.

It was a tiny kitten, its eyes just open. He had found it lying in his garden in a brown paper bag.

He had taken it to the vet, who said it would need feeding every two hours, and had provided special powdered milk, a feeding bottle and written instructions.

The kitten was stripy, with white paws. It was very thin, and the breath fluttered in its throat.

"No-one but you has time, Kane," his grandfather said. "Just think, you can feed it; and when it's a big cat, it will still be yours. Its life is in your hands."

He filled the bottle with warm milk, and held the kitten in his huge, brown hand.

Kane watched it suck life into its body; watched the small paws clench and unclench and heard the small, rusty purr.

"It needs warmth, Kane," his mother said. "I'll bring a thick towel and it can cuddle against you. Nobody else has time to sit with the poor mite."

The kitten pushed its head hard against Kane's hand.

He lay watching it, watching the breath come and go in the tiny body; watching the thin tail, the minute paws, the small, trembling movements. It was so tiny.

It *needed* him. Something no-one else did . . .

WITHIN two days the kitten was Kane's kitten. A passionate desire to keep it alive had taken over his mind, removing all his previous apathy. His father made a bath of warm water, which stored the bottles of milk for the night. Kane set his alarm for every two hours. He could sleep between whiles by day as well as night.

The kitten thrived.

It fed, ever more eagerly, taking more and more food. It began to toddle, making Kane laugh as it tried to walk across the boy's body, often falling.

Then it began to walk well, and within a week scampered all around the bedroom.

Kane played with it, pulling a piece of string for it to pounce on and catch. It slept, as a matter of right, in his arms, cuddled under his chin.

It learned to climb down his blankets to the floor and chase the sunlight; to tease at his hands, and to race after a ball of paper that Kane threw from his bed.

It brought light and laughter to the room.

Then, one morning, when Kane's father was at the office, his sister at school, and his mother had gone shopping, the kitten swarmed up the curtain and from there jumped to the mantelpiece. And there it was marooned.

It was so far to the ground.

It cried. Kane called for his mother but no-one answered. He remembered she had come in to say she would be out all morning and would he be all right?

Of course he'd be all right, he'd said, and had gone on throwing paper balls for the kitten.

Now the kitten was terrified. Its panic grew. It cried to Kane to help it. Kane was there, but unable to move.

The doctor said he could move. The specialist said he could move. His parents said he could move.

Only his obstinate brain said he could not.

He couldn't bear the thin, frightened mews the kitten was making.

Kane pushed back the bed-clothes, and slid to the edge of the bed.

Using his arms to cling to the bed-frame, he rolled to the floor. He swam across the room, clinging to anything that held his weight, pulling himself across the carpet with his arms, crawling as a baby crawls with its very first efforts.

It seemed such a very long way.

There was an armchair beside the mantelpiece. Kane pulled himself up by the arms, and then levered himself into a standing position, leaning against the back of the chair.

He lifted the kitten, and held it tightly.

He had never heard anything like its fervent purr of thanks for its rescue.

He eased himself round the chair; first one leg, then the other, slowly, painfully, long unused muscles rebelling, until he dropped into its cushioned depths and sat, breathless. The kitten slept.

"I can stand," he said, when his mother came home and stared at him, still in the armchair. "The kitten got stuck and I had to help him. I've been looking for a name for him. I think I'll call him Walker."

Twelve years later, when Walker was an elderly cat and lay quietly in the sun, Kane told the story of his kitten to his own small son. "And did you walk back to your bed?" the small boy asked. "It took a long time to learn to walk again," Kane answered.

His voice lifted suddenly and he laughed.

"Come on, let's have that game of cricket. This time you'll be able to hit the ball; and one day, you'll be a county cricketer. It takes time, that's all."

After the game was over he lifted Walker from the patch of sunlight, and carried him indoors, to put him in his bed.

The old cat stretched himself and licked his master's hand. He would never know that he had worked a small miracle. ∎

The Guardian

by Joyce Stranger

Inspired by an illustration by Mark Viney

Clattering hooves and a shattering bray
The donkey greets the break of day
In the farmyard nearby the white geese stray.

When dark he shelters beneath the trees,
Reads news borne on the evening breeze
Sees strange sights that no man sees.

Night!
Chill is the wind and the red fox is running.
Wise are his wiles and his ways are most cunning.
Crouched in long grass the furred hunter is creeping.
Eyes watching the reeds where the white geese lie sleeping.
Leap!
Hard hooves thunder upon the ground.
The intruder is startled by a braying sound.
Swift on the ice his paws are slip sliding,
Past the dead rushes where the farm geese are hiding.
Startled they wake, hear the tell-tale ice crackle.

White wings thresh the air and harsh goose voices cackle.
They fly to the fields and huddle there, quaking.
Out on the lake the thin ice is breaking.
Splash!
The red fox is hungry, his dense fur is soaking.
Ice cold is the water inside his lung, choking.
He crawls up the bank at the red sky's first dawning,
Slinks dejectedly home and sleeps through the morning.

Clattering hooves and shattering brays,
Joyfully frisking, the grey donkey plays,
His charges all safe for many more days.

CUSHION

Cushions add a touch of softness and comfort to any room in the house and create a relaxing, welcoming environment. Our easy project features a practical square cushion made with decorative fabric ties. We used two complementary fabrics — lime check and cobalt blue check — but if you prefer you could use up odds and ends of fabric.

IT!

WHAT YOU'LL NEED
◆ cushion pad ◆ tape measure ◆
fabric for cushion cover ◆ tailor's
chalk ◆ dressmaking scissors or
pinking shears ◆ fabric for piping
and ties ◆ piping cord ◆ basting
thread ◆ pins ◆ sewing machine ◆
matching thread ◆ iron

1 Measure the cushion pad. Allowing 2 cm (¾ in.) extra all round, measure and mark up two squares of fabric using tailor's chalk, and a smaller piece 6 cm (2⅜ in.) long and the same width as the squares for the flap. Cut out the pieces with dressmaking scissors. Then cut out contrasting fabric for the piping; this should be 4 cm (1¼ in.) wide and as long as the outer edge of the cover.

2 To make the piping, fold the contrasting strip in half lengthwise and place piping cord into the fold. Run a basting stitch through the fabric and cord to hold it in place. Then pin this around the edge of one of the fabric squares, raw edges matching, and machine stitch in position.

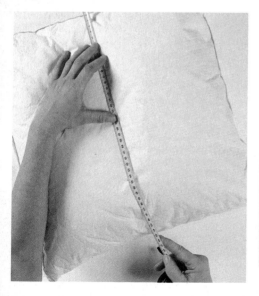

143

CUSHION IT!

3 To make the cushion ties first cut out four pieces of contrasting fabric 20 cm (8 in.) long and 10 cm (4 in.) wide. Fold each piece lengthwise with right sides facing, then turn under the raw edges, and baste and machine stitch around the three sides. Turn the ties the right way out and press with a warm iron to neaten.

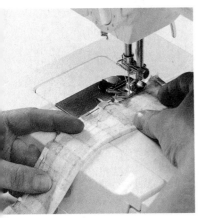

5 Match up the remaining ties on the edge of the piped fabric square; pin in place. Place the small flap of fabric over these ties against the edge of the square, right sides facing, enclosing the ties. Pin, baste and machine stitch the layers together to create an envelope-type flap.

6 Place the other fabric square on top of these layers, right sides together and the ties matching. Pin, baste and stitch around the remaining three sides of the cushion cover. Turn the cover the right side out through the flap. Insert the cushion pad and arrange the ties to finish.

4 Turn under and stitch one edge of the unpiped fabric square. Place two ties on this edge. Baste, then machine stitch in place.

Fool To Cry

Where the man she loves is concerned, not even the most sensible girl will listen to reason.

by
Josefine
Beaumont

B Y the time I was 16, my mirror told me I hadn't got it. A girl's either got it or she hasn't and I, unfortunately, fell into the latter category. To begin with I was, what is commonly termed in the North, a strapping lass. A strapping lass is a polite expression for big and fat.

Why didn't you diet? You ask me. Well, you know how they say that in every fat girl there's a thin girl struggling to get out?

It may be true, but with being a strapping lass you can take away the fat but not the bones. And bones were my problem — big bones.

Still, being a sensible sort of girl, I abandoned the diets and accepted with fairly good grace all that God in His wisdom had given me.

To make matters worse, I must confess that I was also the clever type. I could change a fuse, mend a flat tyre, cook up a storm and swim like a fish.

All this was well and good but it didn't impress the men, I can tell you.

"You're too clever for your own good," Mum warned me time and time again.

Sensible Sarah, that was me.

I dated, of course. William Brownlow even wanted to marry me. I refused. I liked him and he liked me but I felt we were two of life's unfortunates and what kind of basis was that for marriage, I ask you?

Anyway, I was in love with Tom Chase.

Tom lived three doors away and I had known him all my life. He was the most beautiful man I had ever laid eyes upon. It seems rather odd to relate to a man in terms of beauty but Tom was just that. He was like some kind of god.

Due to his excess of good looks he was, as to be expected, always surrounded by a bevy of beauties. They drifted in and out of his life and they were all quite delectable, I can assure you.

It's hard being in love with a man that resembles a Greek god. Still, I was sensible enough, or so I told myself, to know I didn't stand a chance.

Even so, that didn't stop me suffering the agonies of jealousy whenever I saw him with someone else.

Yet, for all that, they were fun years, these years before our 20s. There was a whole crowd of us. I wasn't excluded. Like many a big girl, I was jolly with it. I liked life. I liked to laugh, to live, to enjoy.

One girl hung on to Tom with grim determination. Her name was Angela Thornton. She was the girl with everything . . . if you know what I mean.

She was everything I was not. She had bright blonde hair and innocent blue eyes. Just the right height and just the right everything else with it.

But then something extraordinary happened. It was at the tennis club tournament and I'd just played a vital game with Tom. To be frank I'd completely wiped the floor with him . . . But instead of walking away, stiff-backed and, like most men, disgruntled, incredibly he bounded over the net and congratulated me.

What I saw in his eyes was admiration. I blinked several times because, to be quite honest, I thought I was imagining it.

THAT was just the beginning. Life after that had a rosy glow as Tom and I became a twosome. We were together, part of the crowd and yet not part. We were a couple and I couldn't quite believe it. I blossomed. I know I did. It didn't lend me any beauty but I most certainly blossomed.

Strangely, as my happiness increased, my confidence diminished together with my hard-earned commonsense.

Sensible Sarah was lost and gone for ever.

What did he see in me? I asked myself, time and time again, staring in the mirror at my ample frame. You're going to get hurt, I told myself over and over again, hoping against hope that I was wrong.

Tom and I drifted into marriage. There were no declarations of love, no moments of great passion. Tom seemed to accept that we would marry and I, so unsure and uncertain and afraid of losing him, held my breath and silently prayed.

Even at the altar I was still wondering what he saw in me.

And then the jealousy began. A woman had only to glance at him — and with his looks he drew many a glance — and I was thrown into a turmoil.

We went to Filey for our honeymoon. Tom wanted to go to Greece but I was terrified of flying. Irrational though it was, I had visions of myself passing out with terror at the airport and drawing attention to my bulk. Then there was the thought of those bronzed bikinied beauties on the beach . . .

So Filey it was, and if there was a heaven upon earth, then I entered it during those two weeks.

The weather was bad, but I rejoiced for there were no bikinis anywhere. It was wonderful.

But the honeymoon ended, we came home and my jealousy began to consume me.

The laughter went out of our lives. The conversation became stilted.

I felt I was losing Tom. He had never been verbose, but now he became downright quiet, and there were times when I would catch him looking at me in a strange, sad kind of way.

WHEN I remember the uncertainties of those years I have to be thankful. With all the suffering I wrought upon myself, we could have drifted apart as easily as we drifted into marriage, had it not been for Angela Thornton.

She adopted a habit of dropping in. She would seat herself at my kitchen table, displaying her perfect body in skimpy clothes.

A woman knows when another woman is after her man and let me tell you, Angela Thornton was after Tom

She would barge into our home, breathless and simpering, playing the helpless female to perfection.

If it wasn't the fuse box that needed mending it was her iron . . . or maybe it was her car which wouldn't start. And all this was accompanied by that age-old fluttering-eyelash routine.

I foxed her there, though. I gathered the remnants of my sensible Sarah image and mended her fuse box myself, and her iron, not to mention her car.

I didn't want Tom in her house. I had a dread that if she ever got him through her door I would never see him again.

I got a bit silly during all of this. What with all the worry, the pounds just fell off me. I tried desperately to improve myself, daubing myself with make-up, crippling my feet in high heels, upon which, I might add, I tottered grimly, my knees bending with the sheer exertion of it all.

I even bleached my hair blonde.

"What have you done to yourself?" Tom asked when he came home from work.

"Don't you like it?" I asked, raising a tentative hand to my peroxided head.

"It's terrible," he said flatly.

I burst into tears.

"I liked you as you were," he told me quietly.

Yet, even then, I didn't believe him.

LOOKING back, I realise I have a lot to thank Angela for. On the one hand, she might have tried to ruin my marriage yet, on the other, she saved it. It had to come to a crunch, of course, and it came at the Tennis Club Christmas Party.

Tom and I had been married for two years by then and very strained years they had been. I was there, of course, in my usual party stance, back to the wall, fixed smile upon my face.

So of course I could see how drunk Angela was becoming.

I couldn't believe the way she was throwing herself about to the beat of the music . . . until she fell down drunk, that was.

I recall feeling horribly embarrassed by this shameful display. And it seemed as though I was the only one who viewed her behaviour in that light because everybody else laughed.

Angela, herself prostrate though she was, was surrounded by most of the men in the room, all offering their assistance.

But when she was hoisted to her feet it was Tom she swayed towards, and his ear into which she whispered seductively, "Will you take me home, Tom? I feel dreadful."

He threw me an agonised look and I said, as matter-of-factly as I could, "You'd better. She can't drive in that state."

I'm no fool. I might be a big strapping lass but I'm not daft. I saw the elbow-nudging that went on amongst the men. The raised eyebrows and the shared glances of the women. I saw the sly knowing smiles.

I crept out of the tennis club with the remnants of my dignity like a tattered cloak about my shoulders.

It was past midnight when I entered our house but all I could do was sit down in the rocking chair and cry.

I cried for all the things I wanted to be and knew I never could be.

I cried because love hurt.

Who said it was beautiful? Love was cruel.

I cried because in that moment of time I hated Tom. Even whilst still loving him . . .

148

And I waited, I waited for Tom to come home.

When Tom eventually entered the kitchen there was only the warm glow of the fire to light the room. Only the dull ticking of the clock and the creak of the rocking chair to break the silence.

"What are you doing in the dark?" he asked.

"Please sit down, Tom," I whispered.

"What is it? What's the matter?" he asked.

"Please, Tom . . ." I cried.

"All right, Sarah, if that's what you want."

I waited until he was seated at the kitchen table. I hadn't planned what I would say. It just came tumbling out.

There is a time for everything and some of what had to be said should have been said years ago.

"You know, Tom," I said softly, "I don't think this house has ever heard the truth. It's a miserable house for all its comfort and I hate it."

"Sarah!"

"I do, Tom, I hate it and I always have because, as I said, it's never heard the truth.

"We've lived off half lies and half truths for years, you and I. Neither saying what we mean. You know, Tom, I found out something today and it's changed me. I found out that I'm pregnant. Me, Sarah Chase, imagine . . ."

"A baby? Sarah . . .?" He half rose from the chair and made to come towards me but I cried, "No, don't come near me. Stay there."

I could see, in the firelight, the wounded look upon his face as he sank back into the chair and replied stiffly, "All right, Sarah."

USING the heel of my foot, I set the chair into motion and it rocked gently. It was oddly comforting, that chair. "You know, Tom," I said quietly, "it's not funny being big and fat and having no looks. It's a painful thing, knowing most men wouldn't give you a second look. Some people think that because you're nothing much to look at you've no feelings like other, prettier girls.

"Well, women like me are just the same as the rest. We bleed when we're cut and we laugh and cry and feel pain. Our feelings get hurt should anyone treat us badly.

"All I ever wanted was a chance of a life with you. It seems that I spent the whole of my life waiting to grow up so that I could marry you.

"But when I did grow up I was big and plain and fat and there was Angela, all curved and rounded and gay and lovely.

"But you married me and I could never quite see why." I took a deep breath. "If you want to go to her then I . . . then I won't stop you. I don't think I could if I tried."

I could hardly believe I had said the things I had. Bared my inner self like that.

There was a long, long silence during which my world stood still. I'd gone and offered the man I loved to someone else.

Then there was a sound. A sound that filled me with pain, for he was laughing. My Tom was laughing.

Then he was out of the chair and kneeling before me. He was taking my trembling hands into his own and holding them fast.

"You silly, silly thing. Listen to me. Listen to me. You thought I wanted that . . . that I was in love with Angela? Oh, Sarah, Sarah, I can't stand her! Do you hear me? I can't stand her!"

My eyes widened.

"But you used to go out with her," I protested.

"Once upon a time, yes. Once, she even, in an odd yet inexplicable way, fascinated me. And she knew it. She knows all about men. Her type always do. Some women are born like that. Born wise if you like.

"And don't forget I was only a lad and flattered by her attentions for, as you say, she's pretty. But there are all kinds of prettiness and hers is all on the surface."

"Then — then you knew she was . . . that she wanted you?" I whispered.

"I knew, Sarah, but I didn't want to know," he told me gently. "She thought because of the past I would fall at her feet like I used to all those years ago. She thought she'd only to beckon and I'd come running.

"She used to play with me like a fish out of water at one time. And, like a fish out of water, I used to dangle at the end of her hook. But you know, Sarah, everybody grows up and when that happened to me, I realised that I didn't even like her — never mind the way she treated me.

"You cannot strip a man's pride and dignity and expect him to like it. Do you understand what I'm trying to tell you?"

"I think so," I replied, eyes blurring.

"I took her home tonight because she was drunk and because she asked me. I wouldn't have refused her in front of the whole club, you know that. But that was the only reason I took her home," he stated firmly.

"She was sick in the car," he continued, "and sick at home, so I cleaned her up and left her on the settee . . . I would have done the same for anyone, Sarah, you have to believe that."

"You see, I thought . . . I thought . . ." But I couldn't bring myself to say out loud what I had thought.

"Oh, Sarah," he shook his head, "do you trust me so little? Listen, love, she's trouble. Trouble follows women like that all their lives. I'm not

150

saying it's all her fault but a greater part of it is.

"In a way it's part of the price she pays for being pretty. You see, she thinks the world owes her something because of her looks." He laughed then, not harshly, but pityingly. "All men should fall on their knees in homage to her. Well it's many a year since I got up off my knees and as long as there's breath in me I'll not go down again . . . except to you, Sarah, except to you.

"The best years and the happiest years have been the ones I've spent with you."

"But we haven't been *truly* happy," I told him in a subdued voice.

"And do you know why?" he asked me gently.

"Because you keep trying to change and I don't want you to, that's why."

M Y eyes searched his face. "But I wanted to be better for you," I told him simply. "Oh, Sarah, you couldn't be better for me. I love you as you are. I thought you knew that."

"How could I, when you never told me?" I snapped back.

"I'm not a man of words, Sarah, you know that."

In the flickering firelight our eyes met. Mine, awash with long-awaited happiness, his, warm with the love for me I had denied ever existed.

"Don't you ever say to me that you're big and fat and plain," he said softly. "To me you're beautiful and always have been. There are all kinds of beauty, Sarah, and yours is the special kind.

"It won't wither with age because your goodness and kindness, laughter and love, will shine through for ever.

"Even when we're both old and wrinkled your beauty will still be there, for all to see."

My world was set to rights.

"Do you know what we're going to do, Sarah?" he suddenly said.

"No." My voice was breathless.

"We're going on a second honeymoon," he stated firmly.

"We are?" My voice rose excitedly.

"We'll go to Greece. Our last chance of a holiday together before our baby comes."

Our baby. It had a nice ring that. Our baby.

Greece. GREECE! That meant aeroplanes. That meant flying. That meant swimsuits on beaches, scanty clothes . . .

"But I'm frightened of flying," I wailed.

"Together, Sarah." He laid his head in my lap. "We can do anything together."

Stroking his crisp, black curls, I replied dreamily, "You know, Tom, when you talk like that, I could fly without a plane."

"If you don't mind, Sarah, we'll use an airline like everybody else," he said gently.

Our eyes met. And then we were laughing. Laughing like we used to in the beginning.

All that was years ago.

Tom and I now have a son and a daughter.

We talk out our worries now. And I love Tom more than ever but I see beyond his looks now to the man he has always been — the man who loves *me*.

Angela still lives near us. The years have not dealt kindly with her and yet, oddly enough, we have become friends. I even feel sorry for her.

She is still the same old Angela. Still stunning. The façade, though, is crumbling a little. The make-up a little heavy, the blonde hair a little tarnished, the clothes somewhat over-tight. And she still flutters her eyelashes. But the look sits oddly upon her 36-year-old face.

She is still chasing a dream . . .

Her iron still breaks. As does her fuse box. Her car refuses to start . . . and these occurrences somehow or other always happen at night.

It must be a lonely time for her when families are sitting together, after a meal, at the end of another day.

And I can sympathise . . .

So, I mend her fuse box. I mend her iron. I even see to her car.

I'm no fool. I'm a big strapping Northern lass, and I'm not daft. ∎

ONE LITTLE TRESPASSER

by D.L. Garrard

But the only damage she caused was to his pride, by trespassing on his land and invading his heart . . .

DANIEL STRATTON put down the pile of wicker baskets and straightened his back slowly, regaining his breath. There had been a time when he could carry the same number of baskets full of raspberries and never weary. But he was getting old, now.

He looked down the neat rows of plants, the berries juicy under the leaves and protective netting. A worthy crop, this year. He could have done with an extra pair of hands to help. Not to mention the bright exchange of words and laughter. If only Nancy . . .

His mouth set firmly under the white moustache. He refused to think about his grand-daughter's disloyalty.

He began to make his way down the rows of raspberries, testing the canes for strength, examining the berries. The hours he had spent here in the garden as a boy, playing cowboys and Indians, ducking and hiding until his father shouted at him to play somewhere else, or he'd break all the bushes.

He chuckled to himself, remembering, and crouched to examine the leaves along the bottom of the plants. Then he touched something so unexpected that he almost lost his balance.

He snatched his hand away from the scuffed sandal, above which a rather grubby white sock crumpled round a sturdy calf.

His astonished eyes travelled upwards over a summery blue dress and with a dizzying moment of déjà-vu, he stammered — "Nancy . . .?"

Nancy, seven years old, crying desolately, hiding herself in the garden after Adrian and Pauline were killed in the road accident, trying to keep her grief to herself with the independence she'd always possessed.

But this child wasn't crying and she was nothing at all like Nancy. She was a thin, blue-eyed pixie of a girl, with a lot of shiny red hair straying on to her cheeks and forehead in little wisps. Daniel stood up.

"What are you doing here?" he demanded. "Stealing my raspberries?"

"No!" she said indignantly. "I'm *finking*!"

He opened his mouth automatically to correct her but she continued, "I never saw raspberries as big as this."

"These are the garden kind," Daniel told her dryly. "They've been well looked after. You won't find raspberries like this in any hedgerow."

He had never talked down to Nancy in all the years he had brought her up, but provoked her into asking questions because that was the way children learned.

This one didn't seem surprised by the same tactics. Her tongue played in the gap where her front teeth should be, considering what he'd said.

"Well," Daniel told her, "I'm about to pick the fruit now. It's probably about time you went home."

She looked up at him, her eyes blue and innocent.

"You've no business here, anyway," Daniel said. "How did you get in? I suppose you climbed over the fence?"

She nodded, looking proud of this achievement rather than ashamed.

"Well, through the front gate this time — the proper way. Go on!" he prompted as she scraped the ground with the toe of her sandal, head down, like a small, indecisive bull.

When she reached the gate he called after her, beset by a sudden sense of responsibility.

"You'll be in Ardale Lane through there. Do you know how to get home?"

But either she didn't hear or didn't answer, for the gate swung closed behind her and by the time he reached it, she had disappeared.

The garden settled into stillness again. It was four o'clock on Friday afternoon. The July sunshine had warmed the earth and the grass, ripening the fruit.

Daniel loved to see the results of early digging and planting when the fruits ripened to maturity. It gave him a sense of fulfilment, of having lived to the full and in co-operation with nature.

His heart had once glowed with pride and love for this house, his inheritance and the blessing of someone to follow him in spite of what had happened to Adrian.

Orchard House and its third of an acre would still stay in the family, with Nancy to care for it. Or so he had thought . . .

Now, thoughts like this brought only melancholy if he allowed them. He stood irresolute on the lawn, which was badly overgrown. But it took all his time and energy to stop the garden running wild.

He felt too weary to continue with the fruit picking. And he still had to decide what to do with the morning's harvest. He had far more than he would ever use.

Other years Nancy had organised everything, and after the initial giving to friends and neighbours she sent boxes to the harvest festival and the local hospital. She had made pies and tarts and jam for themselves and the coming fairs.

With a frustrated feeling that he was, somehow, doing this pointlessly, Daniel carried the fruit indoors, a basketful at a time.

Orchard House was really two farm cottages made into one, each half of it a mirror image of the other.

His great-grandfather had bought the cottages with plans for a large family which hadn't materialised.

Daniel's only son, Adrian, had brought his bride home as Daniel had wished. Pauline was a compliant, home-loving girl, and they had occupied one self-contained half of Orchard House.

Daniel had been so pleased and proud. They'd all been happy then.

NOW, he put down a basket stained red with juice and met Nancy's smiling eyes as he straightened. The photograph on the mantelpiece had been taken three years ago on her nineteenth birthday.

She was very like Pauline, the same sweet, oval face, loose tumbling brown hair — but with Adrian's intelligent hazel eyes.

It had taken a long time for Daniel to acknowledge the fact that Nancy was not the sum total of her parents, but an individual. At times she seemed so unlike either of her parents Daniel found her impossible to understand.

Of all the men she could have chosen to marry, Nancy had picked Bradwell Slade.

They had married less than two months after she first brought him home. Now they were living near his parents on the other side of the Atlantic.

But more than that, it was plain to Daniel that during the seven months Bradwell Slade had already spent at the firm he and Nancy worked for, they had become more than casual friends. He was hurt that Nancy had never even mentioned his name before, had kept this man and her feelings for him a secret from even Daniel.

"Bradwell? What sort of a name's that, anyway?" Daniel had muttered when he'd gone. This childish criticism, in fact, was the only one he could find.

Bradwell was presentable, friendly and humorous.

He had an answer for everything and cleverly turned aside any comment of Daniel's which might have led to disagreement.

So cleverly in fact, that Daniel had uneasy suspicions. It was almost as if Nancy had briefed him for the meeting so that it would go smoothly.

What had she told Bradwell Slade — and why?

"Bradwell is a family name," Nancy had said, smiling pleasantly. But her bright eyes had flashed a warning he couldn't ignore.

O N Saturday, Daniel decided he had better pick the best of the strawberries before they rotted away or the wasps devoured them. He'd take a couple of punnets to Reg Wooton at the Red Lion tonight. He couldn't lug whole boxes around, he'd no car.

He didn't like modern gadgets, even resisting Nancy's plea for a telephone. He didn't like them — people could come to the door, he said, instead of just ringing up. And anyway, though he could never admit it, he was slightly deaf.

"I could ring you — if I should be away," Nancy had persisted the last time. He had seen that she was already planning to leave and stubbornly refused to salve her conscience.

There weren't that many strawberries this year. The plants, like him, were getting older. He quickly cleared the strawberry beds and turned back to the rows of raspberries he'd left yesterday.

As he did so, he caught a flash of white from the bottom of a leafy row.

Today the child wore blue shorts and a white T-shirt with Mickey Mouse sprawled across it. She looked up at him and he stared down at her, arms akimbo.

"I haven't *fort* yet," she sighed plaintively, knowing she was about to be evicted.

"Whatever it is you're thinking about, it's taking a long time," Daniel said tartly.

She nodded. "Mummy's finking as well," she volunteered, as if this were an extenuating circumstance.

Daniel had a ludicrous vision of an adult-sized duplicate perched alongside among the raspberry canes and a reluctant smile twitched his lips. Instantly her face creased into a gamine grin which extended almost to her ears.

"I knew you weren't *really* a growly bear, else you wouldn't frow crumbs to the birds. I saw you!"

"*Throw,*" Daniel exclaimed. "*Think*! You're old enough to speak the Queen's English properly!"

She giggled "It's 'cause of my teef! Mummy says I *splutter*! And Rod said . . ."

She sobered suddenly as if speaking of Rod had reminded her of something else.

"Why is it necessary to sit in my garden in order to think?" Daniel queried.

"There's nowhere else I can be private."

"Your own garden?"

"We haven't got one."

"Well, I'm afraid you're going to have to move again," Daniel told her firmly. "Come on, away from there. You can take some strawberries home with you. You won't find any like these in the shops."

She came reluctantly towards him. Plainly the fruit was not a great inducement.

"Have you any brothers or sisters?"

She shook here head.

"Take three punnets then — one each for you and Mummy and Daddy. Come up to the house, I'll find you a bag."

She trotted alongside across the lawn. "I haven't got a daddy, 'zactly," she said pensively.

Daniel felt a twinge of the old intuition which used to tell him Nancy wanted to talk things out. So she didn't have a father. And what, in fact, was all this thinking about?

"Who is Rod?" he asked tentatively.

"He might be my daddy soon. Mummy's finking about it, she said."

HE glanced down and met the question in her upturned face. The sanctuary of his jungle of raspberry canes hadn't been of much use in the matter. She still didn't know what she thought about the idea. "Do you like Rod?"

She nodded positively. "But . . . it would be diff'rent. When he goes home, it's the same as always, me and Mummy playing games and doing fings . . .

"And we'd have to go and live with Rod 'cause he's got two rooms and we've only got one and a bit of kitchen. I don't know if I *want* my own room, by myself . . ."

Daniel sighed. He had always taken his plentiful space for granted. Perhaps wrongly.

"Where do you live now?" he asked her.

"In a room upstairs in Mrs Branby's house. We've made it nice. I've got drawings over my bed, I'll do one of you wiv your ladder. What's your name, so I can put it on the bottom? I'm Lisa."

He told her, rather shaken by the limitations she reeled off so matter-of-factly.

"Look for the good things in life, Lisa," he told her gruffly. "And don't be scared of change. The bigger you get, the more space you'll need.

"You'll have two people to care for you instead of one. If your mummy thinks it's a good idea, I wouldn't hesitate if I were you."

They had reached the back door and Lisa's mouth fell open.

"Is *all* this your house?" she asked, amazed.

"It used to be two houses."

Somehow, her amazement made him feel guilty.

"Is your little girl here?" Lisa asked.

"My little girl?"

"You fort I was Nancy."

"That's Nancy," he said shortly, nodding at the photo. "My grand-daughter. She's married and a long way away."

"How long away?"

"You mean, how *far*? Across the sea." He wished he hadn't mentioned anything now.

"I'd like to go over the sea. Mrs Branby's Alex is in 'Stralia, he sent her a wood kangaroo. She's saving to go and see him —"

"Here are the strawberries," Daniel cut in. "Tell your mother if she wants some raspberries she's welcome to call. But not over the fence!"

Lisa ran off, giggling.

As he left the room, Nancy's eyes pleaded at his back, her voice seeming to take up where Lisa had left off.

"It's a small world now, Grandad. We'll come over, and we'll gladly pay for you to visit us," she had said.

"The world's not so small that I'd see you many more times. I'm over seventy. And I could pay my own fare — If I cared to come. As if there weren't enough local boys —!"

"Brad isn't the first man I've brought home," Nancy had said quietly. "But none of them were good enough for me . . . or rather, for you and Orchard House.

"I've tried to explain, Grandad — I can't spend my life here and it's not reasonable to expect my future husband to, just as a matter of course. But you won't listen —"

"Are you criticising me for asking questions? Your father would have done the same!"

"I know it's because you love me — but you want me to marry on your terms. And you can be a bit of an ogre, Grandad," she said wryly, trying to make him smile.

"You're saying I frightened them off? They wouldn't have allowed that if they really loved you!"

"This one does. And I love him in a different way to the others. It may seem to you that we rushed into it, but we're both sure. Oh, please be happy for me, Grandad! I'll write, often."

*　*　*　*

Between Nancy's photo and the silent clock was a pile of unopened letters. He had dropped the first one there in an act of defiance, still hurting.

He'd been involved in the wedding willy nilly, obliged to smile and act out the part because he didn't have it in him to upset Nancy in front of her friends, or display his own hurt.

But he refused to tear open that letter like a starving man looking for crumbs. She couldn't make him do that. He still had his pride.

When another arrived before he'd read the first, he dropped that on top. One a month almost to the day they came, straight from the doormat on to the mantelpiece.

He couldn't bring himself to read about the life she preferred from the desert of his loneliness.

If she sounded happy he'd feel even more bereft. If she didn't, then he couldn't bear it.

THE rain began late Saturday afternoon. Daniel was soaked going to the Red Lion. Even Saturday with a bit of chat to Reg and watching the darts from the corner seat by the open fire had lost its savour. It was knowing Nancy wouldn't be there when he got home, or at least coming in from her own pursuits with a bright, "Grandad? I'm home!"

The deluge continued all through Sunday and on Monday it was still raining. Five weeks instead of four had gone by since the last letter from Nancy had dropped onto the mat. It would come today, he told himself.

He waited subconsciously for the rattle of the letterbox, and when he heard it just after 10, he deliberately stopped to inspect a potted plant before going into the hall to pick up the letter.

There was nothing on the mat. He experienced such a shock of dismay that he continued to stare, transfixed, at the empty floor.

In that awful moment he knew that Nancy meant far more to him than Orchard House and his hurt feelings. And the letters, in spite of being unread, were a lifeline.

Suppose she had given up on him? Suppose . . . suppose if he did write now, she wouldn't answer?

Another rattle of the knocker made him realise there was someone outside. Two people huddled together under the porch, arms linked and fingers entwined.

"Mr Stratton?" The young woman smiled. "I'm Joanne Selby, and this —" she glanced up at the lanky man with the likeable grin "— is my fiancé, Rod Harris. You've met my daughter, Lisa."

Daniel would have guessed who she was from the pixie face and long red hair. With an effort he pulled himself together.

"You'd like some raspberries? Come in, out of the rain."

"That's very kind of you, but we didn't really come for raspberries," she explained.

"I've mainly come to apologise. Lisa confessed she'd been over your fence twice, but I think we've managed to convince her that she shouldn't do it again. Thanks for being so tolerant — and for the strawberries. They were delicious!"

"I'd plenty to spare. And there's plenty of room in the garden, too. Lisa's welcome to play here," Daniel heard himself say.

It was an admission that sending her away had been just a conventional reaction. He had enjoyed her company really.

"That's very generous of you," Rod said. "Hopefully it won't be too long before we can start looking around for a small place with a garden."

"I'd hoped to make it before we got married, but I'm afraid it's rooms for a while yet."

"We've just been to make arrangements for the wedding," Joanne confided shyly, obviously dying to tell someone.

"Congratulations," Daniel said. "If you've a car, you could take away some fruit as an advance wedding present!"

"I've a van," Rod told him. "Lisa talked about your fruit garden — and I was wondering if you'd care to come to some — er, arrangement?" He looked down, embarrassed. "I've a market stall you see, and I can always sell local produce."

Daniel looked at the eager young man and a bright new idea blossomed in Daniel's mind.

Even though Nancy didn't totally share his feelings for Orchard House, it was still more than just bricks and mortar.

It had known love and it was meant for a family. The garden needed children's voices to bring it alive. There was still a way Daniel could be part of that, if he offered to let half the house to this young couple . . .

"That sounds like a good idea to me, young man," he said. "Why not sit down and I'll make us all a pot of tea while we talk things over? I've a proposition of my own to make."

The postman came up the path as they were leaving, a familiar airmail envelope in his hand. Daniel took the letter with a feeling of such thankfulness that it left him weak.

Everything was all right. Here in his hand he held the key to a whole new world Nancy wanted to share with him and suddenly he felt he'd lots to tell her. He waved to Rod and Joanne, his two new neighbours, then went back indoors. He had quite a bit of reading to do, if he was going to read every one of those letters from Nancy . . . ■

"DON'T LET ME DOWN!"

by Audrey E. Groom

"Face up to things," his dad had told him, "whether it's a bully or a battle." But this was different. This was betrayal!

JEM was curled up on a branch of the old apple tree. He could hear very well his mother calling to him, but he wasn't going to answer. It would cause less trouble in the long run, he had decided, if she didn't find him.

But, of course, he hadn't bargained on Sandie, their large rough collie, coming out into the garden at that point.

She always knew where he was, whenever he hid, and now, as usual, having located him, she stood under the tree, wagging her tail excitedly and barking.

"Go away, Sandie . . ." he hissed. " . . . go on. Go chase a cat or something." But it was too late, for now he heard his mother's voice call up to him yet again.

"Jem, will you please come down. It's far too wet for tree climbing. And I want to talk to you."

Jem sighed. He'd been found . . .

Slowly, he climbed down.

When he reached the ground he leant down to fondle Sandie, who was now leaping around him, still loth to obey his mother. But suddenly she appeared at the back door and said with more urgency: "Oh, do come along, Jem!" And at last, hands in pockets and with the glum expression on his face that his father called "stubborn", he mounted the two steps into the kitchen.

His mother was rinsing cups at the sink now and she turned as he appeared and said, "Oh, there you are, Jem. I thought we'd pop into Sunford this afternoon and get you some new trousers. I wondered if you'd like cords this time. Brown ones, perhaps?"

Jem didn't answer immediately and his mother went on.

"I'd better measure you first, though. See if you've grown at all."

"I don't want new trousers, Mum," Jem said at last, defiantly.

She smiled at him. Her special *I love you, Jem,* smile.

"But you must have some new trousers, love, for your grandad's wedding."

"I'm not going!" Jem could feel his face getting pink. "I've told you . . .!"

"Oh, Jem, love!" She smiled again. "I know you have. But you didn't mean it, did you?"

Jem gritted his teeth. He knew his face was quite red now. He loved his mum and hated arguing with her, but he couldn't help it this time.

"I did mean it." He could feel the tears coming to his eyes.

His mother studied him for a moment, unsure how to go on. And then at last she said: "But, Jem — you'll be letting Granpy down, if you don't come."

But he's let me down, Jem wanted to snap back. Those tears that he considered no longer allowed now he was nine, were dangerously near. They always were lately, when he thought about his grandad.

JEM had always been close to Granpy (hence the special name) even when Granny had been alive. She'd been a very frail lady who had been ill in bed for most of the time that Jem could remember her.

But he had liked going there to help his grandad run the small cottage at the other end of the village.

At that time, his mother occasionally worked in the village shop, so she was only too pleased that Jem was happy with his grandfather.

They were wonderful days, going shopping together, Jem's hand clasped in Granpy's. Or washing up, with Jem standing on an old box to reach the sink. And playing with the water and old cups long after the washing up was finished.

Granpy never minded how much mess he made. It was the same with cooking.

Then three years ago his granny had died, only a few months before his little sister was born. So although his mum didn't work at the shop any more, she was still very busy with Ruthie.

And so Jem spent more time than ever with Granpy now that he was alone.

Lately, with Sandie trotting beside them and packets of sandwiches in their pockets, they would spend long days fishing, swimming, or just walking the green hills.

And in the winter, Granpy and he would sort out their stamp collections together in the warm little living-room of the cottage, or watch Westerns on TV, or play Snakes and Ladders.

Yes, it had all been lovely, until just after Hallowe'en when Granpy had gone up to London for a couple of weeks to stay with Jem's Uncle Paul and his wife.

And there he'd met Dorothy. Now, for some stupid reason, they had decided to get married. And they actually expected Jem to go to the wedding and be pleased.

Pleased! How could he be pleased, when not only was Granpy introducing a complete stranger into their close, wonderful little world, but he was also leaving the village, where he and Jem had had such marvellous times together.

How could he?

Obviously Granpy didn't care about all that — or even *him.*

As usual, however, when his mother mentioned "letting Granpy down", he felt miserable and hurt inside. And he couldn't prevent one tell-tale tear trickling down his face.

He knew he was too old to be cuddled, like a baby, by his mother. But it was still nice when she did it — as now, for instance.

"You haven't talked to Granpy about this, have you, Jem?" she said, drawing away and wiping his cheek with a tissue.

He hung his head. "No, Mum."

"Or been to see him for ages?" she went on.

"No."

It was true. Ever since that terrible evening just before Easter when Granpy had brought Dorothy to share their evening meal and told them, "We're getting married soon," Jem hadn't been along to Granpy's cottage at all.

And on the few occasions when Granpy had come to their house, Jem had managed to be out with the Scouts, or across the road at his friend, Tom's, home.

Weekends and after-school had been dull because of it. But then, if his grandad could forget all their good times together just for some silly woman that he hardly knew, what could you expect?

Still, I'll manage without him, Jem had thought defiantly. But he wasn't going to the wedding, on that he was quite determined.

"Well, I tell you what, Jem —" Mum was getting her cake box down now, "— we won't bother about your trousers today, after all. You go along and see your grandad instead and have a talk to him. I'm sure he's missed you these last weeks.

"Oh, and take this cake with you, love. Granpy's too busy packing and sorting to bake any for himself at the moment."

"Mum, I don't want —" Jem was worried now.

"Look, Jem." His mother crouched down on the floor in front of him. "You know what your dad always tells you about not running away from problems?"

Jem nodded. He knew very well.

"Face up to it, lad," his dad always said. "Whether it's a bully or a battle — it doesn't do any good to run away, Jem."

But this was different, wasn't it? It wasn't a bully or a battle but — a betrayal. He knew all about betrayals — he'd asked his dad what it meant when he'd heard it on TV.

And he wasn't at all sure he wanted to talk to his grandad about it. But his mother wasn't going to let him away with it, obviously.

"Off you go, then, Jem," she said brightly, putting the plastic box of cake into his hands.

"Give Granpy my love, and be back for tea, won't you? Bring him with you if he'd like to come."

JEM frowned and tucked the box under his arm. In the hallway he passed his small sister sound asleep in her pushchair, her dark curls tumbling over the round, pink face, flushed with sleep. Nice to be three years old, he thought loftily. You didn't have problems at three. You could just sleep the afternoons away and wake up and smile and everything was fine.

Mind you, he wouldn't have wanted her to have anything to worry about. He would have fought anyone who hurt or upset her in any way.

Yes — she was all right, his little sister. He was glad he had her. Mum and Dad and Ruthie and himself — it was a nice, cosy feeling being part of a family.

But as he walked through the village he forgot Ruthie and his thoughts went straight back to Granpy and what he was going to say to him.

But as he neared the cottage, his steps slowed.

Only a few months ago he had run along this road, battered on the kitchen door and ran in calling, "Granpy, Granpy, it's me, Jem."

But today he didn't rush or call out.

Today Jem crept in quietly and through to the small living-room and then just stood looking.

It wasn't tidy as Jem remembered it. There were piles of books everywhere, some on the table, some on the floor, some still on the bookshelves.

And Granpy was sitting looking at a photograph album.

Jem coughed and Granpy looked up with a sad look on his face which was replaced instantly by a wide smile.

"Oh, Jem! I'm so pleased to see you, laddie. I've missed you — thought you'd forgotten your old grandad."

Jem stood awkwardly, looking down at his feet. Normally he would have run to his grandfather and been enfolded in a big bear-hug.

Now he was tongue-tied — didn't know what to do or say. His grandad saw this and looked back down at the photos as if he didn't know what to say, either.

At last Granpy closed the album and coming over to him put a hand on his shoulder.

"I'll make us some tea, shall I, Jem? No rock cakes, though, I'm afraid." He waved a hand around him. "Been too busy, I'm afraid, and, er —" his voice dropped "— I've had no-one to share them with."

"Mum sent some cake," Jem mumbled, presenting the box.

"Oh! Good! I'll cut us some, then." Granpy went out to the kitchen and Jem heard the chink of tea-cups.

He moved over to the window, where his grandad had put the photo album down on a coffee table. Jem sat down and opened it and began to turn the pages.

Most of the pictures were of a very beautiful lady in old-fashioned clothes, whom he didn't recognise at all. He was still looking at them when Granpy came back with the tray.

"Do you like my old photos, Jem?" he said. "They're early ones of your granny, you know. Wasn't she lovely?"

But Jem only frowned as he watched Granpy.

Suddenly he wondered if Granny-in-Heaven was angry that Granpy was marrying another lady.

HIS grandad pushed tea and cake across to him. "I really am pleased you've come, Jem," he said. "I mean, we've always been such good pals, haven't we? I hope that's not going to change." Jem looked up and Granpy was staring straight at him — right into his very heart. And his eyes were asking the questions, *Why haven't you been to see me, Jem? What have I done?*

Jem played with his cake. He didn't feel like eating it, somehow. He didn't feel like talking, either, but he knew he had to, or there was no use in him coming here.

"What's wrong, Jem?" Granpy said, following up his other questions. "I did hear a rumour that you don't want to come to the wedding. Is that right?"

Jem nodded and took a deep breath.

"Why, lad?"

Jem shrugged, and then meeting the older man's eyes, the words all came out in a rush.

"'Cause I don't see why you want to get married and go away and leave us."

Having said it all, he blushed furiously and took a gulp of tea.

He could hear his grandad's teaspoon clinking in the cup as he stirred, but he couldn't look at him. Instead, he stared down at the steam rising from the tea.

Then Granpy said, "Well, of course, I know we're going to miss each other. We had good times, didn't we?"

Jem nodded, not trusting himself to speak again yet.

"Yes, they were great," his grandad continued, and sat for a few moments as though thinking back on them. Then he went on, "Of course, I was a bit lonely when you were at school, you know — and when you were out playing football with Tom on Saturday afternoons.

"Then there was that terrible long week when you went off to Scout camp."

Jem frowned again. It hadn't occurred to him to wonder what his grandad did when he wasn't there.

"Yes," he said, "I s'pose."

"Mmm," Grandad went on, "I often feel a bit lonely at night, too.

"Of course, you're lucky there, aren't you? I mean, you've got Ruthie in the next room and your mum to come and tuck you both in. And if you wake in the night — well, they're all there close to you, aren't they?"

JEM sat, thinking about what his grandad was saying. Things that he had never thought about before. "Of course," Granpy continued now, "it was different when your granny was alive. Even though she was ill, we still had a lot of happiness. We were together."

And suddenly the thought that Jem had had a few minutes before about his granny surfaced again and he asked: "But wouldn't she mind, Granpy, that you're marrying someone else? Wouldn't she?"

"Mind?" Granpy looked surprised. "She loved me, Jem. It's what she would have wanted for me. If you love someone, you want them to be happy, don't you?"

Well, now — that was another thought that hadn't occurred to him.

Jem was feeling more and more mixed up. There was something else that he had to know, though.

"But why do you have to go to London, Granpy — couldn't you still live

here?" he asked.

"Well, to be honest, Jem," answered his grandad, "I'd rather we were going to stay here. But Dorothy's house is bigger and she has a disabled sister to look after and there wouldn't be room here."

"But don't you mind leaving?"

Grandad nodded. "Yes, I do, Jem," he said. "But then I love Dorothy, so I don't want to make problems for her, do I?"

Like I've been doing for you, Jem thought, and somehow he didn't feel so cross any more, more sorry really, that he had got it all wrong.

In fact, he had a horrible feeling that he was the one who was being selfish. He raised his eyes to see his grandad smiling at him — the old, warm *we're the best of buddies* smile.

And, suddenly, all the long, hurting weeks were washed away and Jem jumped up from his chair.

"Oh, Granpy!" he said, and there didn't seem to be any need for more conversation as two strong arms went around him and held him tightly.

That made everything seem right and bright.

"Will you come back to tea with us, Granpy?" Jem asked. "Mum said to bring you."

"That'll be great!" Granpy answered. "I was wondering what I was going to have to eat tonight. I've got a little low on shopping lately. Perhaps we could do it together, tomorrow, Jem."

"Mmm, all right." Jem felt happier than he had for weeks. "And you could come with us to get my new trousers for the wedding, couldn't you, Granpy?

"Mum says brown ones would be nice, but brown's not a very happy colour, is it?

"I think I'd like red . . ."

"You can have green and white striped, if you like . . ." Granpy said, happily.

"Oh, no, Granpy." Jem was horrified. "They wouldn't be nice at all!" ■

THE SEAL PUP'S LULLABY

by Joyce Stranger

Inspired by an illustration by Mark Viney

Swiftly swoop and swing through the combers.
Dive through the blue-green glass clear waters.
Swim deep, where the fronded sea-weeds waver.
Drift where the sea's fast currents wander.
Bask on grey rocks when the bright day is dawning.
Chase glinting fish through the sun-flecked shallows.
Lunge on ribbed sands when the ebb tides are flowing.
Hide when grown seals are in the bay courting,
Leaping and plunging and gaily disporting.
Creep up the beach when the wild storm winds rampage,
Avoid death-dealing rocks and the sea's sullen rage.
Play with your cousins when the beach is deserted.
Learn mankind is cruel and hide from his coming.
Keep out of the path of the stern Beach Master.
Lie close and sleep 'neath the seal mother's flipper.
Sleep, little pup. Gain strength for tomorrow.

On The Wings

ELAINE sits on the small harbour beach leaning against the wall, head raised to the September sun. There are scattered families dotted about the beach, picnicking in the sun, laughing, sunbathing, enjoying themselves.

The children near her have names like Jerome and Portia and George. They all look under five and the mother is very young and earnest.

Elaine smiles to herself, wondering how many books influenced her choice of names.

The scene is familiar, as much a part of Elaine as breathing. She lived here all her life, until two years ago.

Her children played on this beach and she with them. How simple life seemed then, how straight and uncomplicated.

She finds herself staring at the young mother. What does life hold for her? What is in store?

There she kneels, building castles of sand with her small children around her, and apparently not a care in the world.

But then, why should she be aware of the shadows that crouch waiting in a life that is both sun and shadow?

·Elaine feels a pang for her, a protective motherly pang, and turns her eyes away to the sea. Loneliness floods through her.

Odd, she thinks, people on their own are rarely lonely, only in a room full of people or a beach full of families are they truly lonely.

She gets up and wanders along the harbour wall, then takes the path to the cliffs until she stands above the long white surfing beach of her childhood and teenage years.

She and all her friends would meet her, summer and winter. Here she had first seen John. In a wet suit, tall and tanned, clutching a surf-board. The Cornish champion, laughing, rushed out into the waves.

Loss floods Elaine once again, but she raises her head, looks out to sea, and shakes away the memories.

Slowly she makes her way down to the beach. Out there in the waves

Of A Dream

by Sara Jane MacDonald

Like the sea, life was constantly changing. So she'd flown off on her own to find out if she could sink or swim . . .

surfers bob like black seals waiting for the right wave, then caught on the crest of one they rise high, high, and fly like beautifully-balanced birds inwards, beachwards, till they tumble to earth in the foamy white surf.

Elaine laughs, capturing their excitement. The sky is now cloudless, so blue against the green cliffs.

Joy at being back explodes inside her. Sheer utter exhilarating joy that has lain dormant, waiting to be released.

She realises in that moment of joy that she will, after all, paint again. Her talent is not dead as she thought, but has been lying sleeping, hibernating, like her joy.

She feels released, something surfaces within her, a feeling that has no words and is an exquisite mixture of pain and happiness. A sweet knowledge that something important to her is not lost.

It is still there, as much a part of her as the grains of sand between her toes. It has just been imprisoned, deadened, by grey buildings and the sound of traffic.

She moves on across the beach, past the Surfing Club where black-clad figures lounge, recovering from the battering of the waves. On to the end of the beach where her rock, flat and smooth, waits in the shelter of the cliffs.

JOHN had never really understood why she could not paint in the city. "Surely," he would often ask, "it can't just be the light that's wrong?" Now, pulling herself up on to the rock, her favourite spot, she smiles up at the sky. Not for nothing is the town full of painters and sculptors. This wonderful light and shade that appears different from anywhere else, attracts so many.

But John is right, it is not just the light.

She should have explained that painting is not just interpreting what you see, it comes from a deep force inside, an expression of love that is subconscious, so much a part of you that observation is only a part of it. She should have explained, but she couldn't.

Not once in that flat in London had she been tempted to pick up her brush.

Her hair has worked loose somehow. She shakes it free of the slide and it tumbles and blows away from her face.

The thought of the flat makes her shiver. Not so bad the first five months when the twins were still at home, but after they left for universities miles away, the shock of the alien landscape became unbearable.

They, knowing it would, worried, urged her out of her homesickness.

"Couldn't you get a job, Mum? If you won't paint, please do something, or you'll go mad."

But John said nothing. John Pascoe, champion surfer, beloved companion, husband of so many years, did not have time to worry about his wife.

PROMOTION had brought big responsibilities. He had worked hard and ambitiously all his life and finally he was running his own show. Power was heady and he revelled in it. There were dinner parties, cocktail parties, company parties, and always, Elaine thought, the same people at all of them, having what seemed like the same conversations.

Elaine was conscious of being and feeling like a fish out of water. And she was aware of John's disapproval, what he saw as her lack of effort on his behalf, lack of sophistication.

172

The way she got through was to look beyond the sea of heads, to transport her mind to the cliff paths and winding lanes, to conjure the smell of mown grass or the smell of fish when the boats came in.

It was the old, old story . . .

He was leaving her behind, forging ahead in his new-found power, not because she was unintelligent or unable to adapt, simply because she was secretly appalled that he should expect her to be something she wasn't.

It hurt to realise that after all these years he knew her so little. And seemed oblivious to the fact that it was simply too late for her to change now.

If she had known how he would change, how it really would be, would she have moved, uprooted herself for him?

Thinking back, she clasps her hands round her knees. I never wanted to go, but he had waited so long for this, my lovely ambitious Cornishman. I couldn't refuse, I had to support him, and I was so proud of him.

But I always thought we believed in the same things. I knew it would be hard to leave Cornwall after a lifetime, but I thought John would be the same. And he wasn't.

And that was the worst thing of all, to see someone change before your eyes.

A seagull is floating on the wind, idling in the shelter of the cliff. Her aunt's voice comes back to her, unusually cross.

"It is no good lifting someone up, tearing their roots out and plonking them down in the unknown, Ellie, saying, 'Get on with it, I'm too busy.'

"You are part of his life, his wife and you gave up your job, your lifestyle, your studio, for him, and he should jolly well help you to adjust . . . Men . . .!"

Elaine grins.

Dear Aunt Anne and your life-long suspicion of men. You have freed me by leaving me the cottage where I grew up, thank you. I owe you everything I am.

Elaine had grown up and lived with her aunt since she was three years old when both her parents had been killed in a road accident.

Now she tries to concentrate on just watching the waves curling in and not to think, but it does not work.

Instead, she remembers John, staying later and later at the office. Business lunches, business dinners. Conferences. Weekend conferences. Slowly, slowly slipping away from her.

It was then she knew, knew without him saying a word that there was someone else and the isolation and pain were immeasurable.

And so Aunt Anne, without knowing it, had provided her escape back to Cornwall.

As she had left London behind, she felt a surge of pure relief that that way of life was over — despite losing John. Despite a long happy marriage until two years ago. Despite still loving John.

But she did not love the London John — not the stranger.

So she will sit here remembering the gentle Cornish giant. Yes, that is how she will insist on remembering him.

Even as she sits, the light is changing, shadows lengthening. She pulls on a sweater.

Better to let go, she tells herself, *remember the good times, then let go. No good clinging to what is no more.*

So why am I crying? Why am I hurting? Why is my sense of loss as endless as that sky?

The light is changing now, mellowing. How wonderful to see the sea change colour before her eyes. How beautiful the world is . . .

She leans forward, gazing at the moving, changing sea and in her mind paints a small clear picture of speckled, subdued waves in early-evening sunshine.

SHE does not hear the footsteps or see the man approaching her. He stands quite still, watching her. He is tall and athletic, but tired looking, a little like the surfers emerging from the sea. "Ellie . . ." He whispers to himself. "The Ellie I know."

She turns quickly then, caught unawares, and he moves to lean against the rock. Neither speaks.

It is a long time since she has seen him out of a suit, in sweater and jeans; he does not seem the London John. And this John is finding the right words difficult.

"Ellie," he says, "I brought the twins with me. All the way down they've been telling me how power corrupts. They're right."

She sees he is gently mocking himself, is unsure, not the confident London John.

"I couldn't believe your letter, couldn't believe you really would leave me. Ellie, without you I'm only half a person; that's not original I know, but it's exactly how I feel."

Elaine looks at him. "John, I'm sorry, but I can't live in London."

"I know you can't." He smiles, suddenly staring at her. "You even look different down here, the same ageless Ellie. I didn't recognise the London Ellie."

"Nor I the London John."

Their eyes meet, and despite all, and because of the strength of the happy years, love is still there. And they both know it.

He climbs up on to the rock. "I had forgotten how good it was to breathe free. How I love this place . . ." He doesn't speak for a long time but when he does it is with fierce determination.

"Ellie, I want to wind down the London job slowly with a view to moving back to my old one.

"It would take some months. Would you have me back, eventually? The time would give you a breathing space."

Before she can answer, there is a yell and the twins appear running down the beach in wet suits, carrying their surf-boards.

Elaine catches her breath, for her son looks exactly like his father years and years ago.